CONNECTED TO THE PLUG

3

B.B.'s Return

DWAN WILLIAMS

Good2Go Publishing

D1361918

CONNECTED TO THE PLUG 3
Written by Dwan Williams
Cover Design: Davida Baldwin
Typesetter: Mychea
ISBN: 3 9781947340114
Copyright ©2017 Good2Go Publishing
Published 2017 by Good2Go Publishing
7311 W. Glass Lane • Laveen, AZ 85339
www.good2gopublishing.com
https://twitter.com/good2gobooks
G2G@good2gopublishing.com
www.facebook.com/good2gopublishing
www.instagram.com/good2gopublishing

Acknowledgments

I would like to acknowledge my good friend Harold Hall Jr. for all of the late nights he put in with me in helping me put this project together. Also Shonda Gray for being the best friend anyone could ask for. Last but not least I would like to acknowledge my family and Good2Go for the support they have given me. Thanks and God Bless.

CONNECTED TO THE PLUG

TO THE PLUG

3

B. B.'s Return

Fuzzy exhaled a breath of relief when she brought her G55 Benz truck to a halt in front of her old residence that she once shared with her deceased husband, Speedy. So many memories resurfaced as soon as she put the truck in park, killed the engine, and looked up at the mansion. Before she even got a chance to say a word, Jr. and Lil Menace jumped out of the back seat and raced into the backyard. Ever since Slim had called and told the boys that their brand new 4-wheelers were out in the back waiting on them, they couldn't wait to reach their destination.

"Y'all be careful out there on those ATVs," Fuzzy called out after them. Just like any other loving and caring mother, she didn't like the fact that Slim had gotten the dangerous machines for the boys, but what could she say? She would eventually have to let them grow up and wouldn't always be able to protect them from the dangers in the world.

On the way up to the mansion, Fuzzy's daughter, Sade, was dead on her heels. Even though Sade was in the middle in age, Fuzzy treated her as the baby, being that she was the only girl. She was so close behind her mom that when Fuzzy stopped to search her handbag for her keys, Sade bumped into her.

"Sorry." Sade smiled as she looked into Fuzzy's eyes. After finding the right key, Fuzzy opened the door and was met by more memories. She was snapped back to the present when Sade brushed past her and headed up the stairs to her old bedroom.

The first thing Fuzzy noticed when she walked into her spacious bedroom was the picture that she and Speedy took together on their wedding day. She made it across the room to where it sat on the nightstand on her side of the bed, then picked it up. "I love you, baby," she whispered, then placed her lips on the picture. Before she was able to put it back on the nightstand, Sade entered the room.

"Mommy," she called out from the doorway.

"Yes, Princess," Fuzzy quickly responded while wiping her eyes. There was one thing Fuzzy tried to keep her children from seeing, and that was her crying. She was their hero, and that's the way she wanted to keep it.

"May I go out back and play in the pool?" Sade asked, her voice filled with excitement.

"Sure you can, sweet—" Fuzzy attempted to say, but Sade was racing down the hallway before Fuzzy could finish her sentence. While Sade took the stairs two steps at a time, Fuzzy was on her way to the double doors that led to the balcony. "Be careful," Fuzzy yelled out below once Sade came into view. When Sade climbed the ladder onto the diving board, she turned to face her mother.

"Look, Mommy." Sade made her way to the edge of the diving board, took one bounce, and then did a frontward flip into the air and ended it with a twist before making a perfect landing. When Sade came up for air, all she could hear was Fuzzy cheering on. Sade loved to make her mother proud of her, and she did every chance that she got. Slim had talked Fuzzy into letting Sade take up swimming as a hobby in hopes of keeping her away from the life that Fuzzy was exposed to at such an early age. Fuzzy rested her elbow against the balcony railing as Sade played around in the pool. Before she knew it, Fuzzy's mind had drifted off to the night she and Speedy first met at a little hole-in-the-wall joint called The Twilight Zone:

"Can I have two glasses of Moscato?" Fuzzy asked. Once the bartender told her the price, she went into her oversized handbag to get her wallet out, but before she could pay for it, Menace intervened.

"Make that a bottle of Moscato for the prettiest ladies in the place," he complimented while staring at Red, who stood in front of him.

"One bottle coming up," the bartender announced, then turned to walk away. Menace chuckled then stopped the bartender before he could make his exit.

"No, you must have misunderstood me, my man." The bartender stood with a confused expression on his face. "I meant a bottle for each one of the ladies." Menace clarified while pulling out a wad of money and removing two one hundred dollar bills to take care of the order. Menace peeped at how Red's eyes lit up before he put the wad back in his pocket. Fuzzy was about to protest, but Red spoke before she could.

"Thank you very much, handsome." She held her hand out so the introductions could be made. "My name is Tammie, but all of my friends call me Red for short," she answered shyly. She found herself lost in Menace's deep gray eyes as she stared into them. He nodded his head in approval as he looked Red up and down. She was dressed in a pair of tight-fitting Dior jeans that seemed to hug each and every one of her many curves, but since Menace was a foot man, her matching open-toe Dior heels immediately caught his eyes. Her red top complemented her brownish-red hair, which made Menace wonder if her pubic hairs were the same color as well. "So can I be one of those friends that call you Red?" Menace flirted and licked his lips.

"I think we might can make that possible," she flirted back. He could tell that she was really feeling his swagger by the way he had her smiling from ear to ear. They stood quietly staring into each other's eyes with dirty thoughts running through their minds before Fuzzy spoke up and broke their train of thoughts.

"Anyways." Fuzzy turned to Speedy and said, "My name is Chantel, but my friends all call me Fuzzy," mimicking her best friend. Speedy shook Fuzzy's awaiting hand then planted a soft kiss on the back of it." My friend can be so rude at times," Fuzzy added as she cut her eyes in Red's direction. Red looked over at her friend and hunched her shoulders then gave Menace her undivided attention.

"Nice to meet you. My friends all call me Speedy," Speedy cleared his throat then replied. He was kind of in a trance at how beautiful Fuzzy was, and she knew it. Being that she stood about five foot five and wore her hair back in a neat ponytail that complimented her almond shaped hazel eyes, not many could overlook her natural beauty. The fact that her measurements were a perfect 36-24-37 didn't hurt either. Any man that knew women could immediately tell that she was high maintenance, and that's what made Speedy want her even more.

"Can I have my hand back please?" Fuzzy smiled but removed her hand before Speedy decided to let it go. Her conceitedness made him grin. The bartender came back with their bottles just in time. Speedy knew it was going to be a task to get Fuzzy, a task that he was most definitely up for. Speedy pulled out a hundred-dollar bill from his wallet and tipped the bartender. After cuffing his tip, he was on his way to the next patrons at the other end of the bar.

"Are y'all lovely ladies chillin' wit us up in VIP tonight?" Menace questioned, pointing at the VIP section of the club. Red looked over at Fuzzy with pleading eyes, letting her know she wanted to chill with the ballers for the night, but the look on her best friend's face let her know that she wasn't really feeling the idea at all.

"We ain't gonna bite," Speed assured Fuzzy and Red and walked off toward the VIP Section before either of them could respond.

"I know he didn't," Fuzzy thought to herself as she watched his departing back make its way through the crowd. "This boy must really be feeling himself." Fuzzy wanted to put him in his place, but truth be told, his arrogance kind of turned her on. The sound of Menace's voice was the only thing that stopped Fuzzy's stare from burning a hole in Speedy's back.

"Well if y'all ladies decide to join us, we'll be in VIP." He gave Red one last charming smile then walked away to give the two ladies some privacy to decide what they wanted to do. As soon as Menace was out of earshot, Red began to plead her case.

"So are we going to chill with them or what?" She secretly had her fingers crossed behind her back. After Fuzzy didn't answer right away, she followed her eyes to see what had her attention. Speedy and Menace had made it into VIP and had their bottles in the air, signaling for them to come over and join them. That only got Red more hyped up. "Do it for me," she pressed, poking out her bottom lip followed by a pout. Fuzzy was never really able to tell her best friend no, and the way Red was batting her eyelashes, she knew that Red knew that she had her eating out of the palms of her hand.

"Come on, girl, damn," Fuzzy cursed then rolled her eyes. "You better be glad I love your stinking behind." Red jumped up and down twice, clapping her hands like a kid in a candy store. "I love you too," Red stated honestly. "You better because . . ." Fuzzy's sentence was cut short when Red grabbed her hand and pulled her toward the VIP Section.

Once they reached the red rope that separated the VIP section from the other partygoers and informed the big bouncer who they were with, he led them to Speedy and Menace's booth. "I see y'all ladies decided to join the fun." Speedy smiled and stood to his feet.

"Don't flatter yourself," Fuzzy shot back and rolled her eyes as she took the seat beside him while Red sat beside Menace with a wide smile on her face. While Speedy and Fuzzy sat quietly sipping on their drinks and watching the people in the club do their thing, Red and Menace were deep in conversation, enjoying each other's company. It wasn't until the DJ put on "In the Club" by 50 Cent that Red grabbed Menace by the hand and pulled him out of his seat.

"Come on, cutie. This my jam," she shouted over the thunderous bass. Speedy had to admit that his partner knew how to handle his own on the dance floor, but truth be told, Red stole the show with all of her exotic moves that she was putting on him.

After three songs Red decided to give Menace a break and return to their booth to check up on their friends." Anyone want another bottle?" Speedy asked after placing the empty bottle of Moet back on the table. Once everyone declined, Speedy gave himself a once over then made his way to the VIP exit. Before the bouncer opened the rope, he spun quickly on his heels and caught Fuzzy gazing at him.

Fuzzy was brought back to reality by the sound of her cell phone ringing on her hip. When she took it off and looked at the display screen, a smile quickly appeared on her face when she saw Shelia's picture and name pop up.

"Hey, Auntie," she sang once she connected the call.

"When are you bringing my great niece and nephews over to see me?" she questioned, getting straight to the point of her call. Shelia hated that Fuzzy had moved to Georgia with the kids because she was not able to see them as much as she wanted to.

"WE will be down to the restaurant in a little while." Fuzzy laughed then began to tell Shelia about their trip home, before promising to have the kids to Big Mama's Kitchen in the next hour. After Fuzzy got Sade in the house to take her shower and get dressed, she headed outside to gather up the boys. It took her thirty minutes, but she was finally able to get the boys off of their 4-wheelers, with the help of them running out of gas. She was glad she was able to talk Slim into only filling the tanks halfway up with gas.

"Where are we going, Aunt Fuzzy?" Lil Menace questioned for the third time since they got in the truck.

"It's a surprise," she responded as she looked into the rearview mirror at him. It amazed her how much Jr. and Lil Menace looked like their fathers (Speedy & Menace).

"What's the surprise?" Lil Menace asked like she knew he would.

Before Fuzzy got the chance to answer, Sade sucked her teeth, rolled her eyes into the back of her head, and snaked her neck. "It wouldn't be much of a surprise if she told us, now would it?"

Jr. reached up from the backseat and pulled one of Sade's ponytails, snapping her head back into the headrest. "Ouch," she screamed, then yelled to Fuzzy to make him stop.

"Alright, Speedy," Fuzzy shouted. "I'm not Speedy, Mommy. I'm Jr." He laughed at his mother for calling him his daddy's nickname.

"Well you know who I meant." Fuzzy shook her head from side to side then reached for the volume on the steering wheel to adjust the volume up a notch. Even though "The Three Amigos," as she sometimes referred to them as, could be a handful, she wouldn't trade any of them for anything in the world.

As soon as Fuzzy pulled into the parking lot of Big Mama's Kitchen, the kids all cheered with joy. It was their favorite place to eat because not only did they get to eat whatever they wanted, but they also got to play as many games in the video game room as they wanted to play. The fact that their Great Aunt Shelia spoiled them with gifts or money whenever she saw them didn't hurt either. "There go my little princess and my nephews." Shelia gleamed with joy when Fuzzy entered the restaurant with the kids in tow. The kids ran up to Shelia and gave her a huge bear hug followed by a kiss on the cheek. After handing them a hundred dollar bill a piece, Shelia led them to a reserved table in the back.

After the kids ordered their food, Fuzzy gave them ten dollars each so they could get change from the machine to play the video games until their food was ready. That would also give Fuzzy and Shelia enough time to catch up on what'd been going on since she'd been gone, as well as the business side of things." So how are you enjoying the condo?" Fuzzy questioned. The smile on Shelia's face said it all.

"Girl, I am loving it. It's so nice and peaceful, not to mention it's in the heart of everything. It's always something different to get into." Fuzzy knew that to be true. That was the main reason she bought it in the first place.

"I'm so glad you like it," Fuzzy stated honestly. Now it was time to get down to business." So how is everything coming along with the restaurant?" Fuzzy studied Shelia's facial expression and noticed her smile slowly fade away as she tried to find the words to explain it.

"Business is good besides the fact that I had to fire the third shift manager for having sticky fingers," Shelia confessed.

"How much was she stealing?" Fuzzy asked, knowing that in the business world, no matter what kind of business it was, someone was always going to be greedy and pinch off the top.

"About a couple hundred a week, and I didn't get hip to her until a month had passed." Fuzzy estimated around eight hundred or so dollars then chalked it up as a loss.

"Don't even worry about it, Auntie. Did you say anything to Uncle Slim about it?"

Shelia shook her head no.

"Good. I'll straighten everything out, and this will be our little secret." Shelia tried to decline, but Fuzzy wasn't trying to hear it. She didn't want Shelia to stress herself over spilled milk. Fuzzy knew that it was about time for the food to arrive and that meant the children would be headed back to the table at any time, so she decided to touch on the main subject before they did. "So how are things really going with you?" The question was so simple, and Shelia knew exactly what Fuzzy was referring to.

"I've never been cleaner," Shelia admitted truthfully. Fuzzy could see the glow of Shelia's skin and the sparkle in her eyes and knew that she was telling the truth. It was at that point Fuzzy knew she had made the right decision by handing Shelia the deed to the restaurant and condo. As if on cue, the waitress, as well as the kids, showed back up to the table at the same time. Fuzzy wanted to let Shelia know how proud she was of her, but the look on Shelia's face let her know that she already knew.

After the kids filled themselves up with food and

dessert, they were back off to the game room. "You know the old-school jamboree at club Drama is tonight, right?" Fuzzy reminded Shelia.

"I hope you have fun," Shelia replied, then took a sip of iced tea.

"We are going to have fun," Fuzzy corrected with hopeful eyes. Shelia almost spit her mouthful of tea all over the table. Shelia was about to speak, but Fuzzy spoke up first."Pleeaassee," she whined with her hands over her heart. Shelia hadn't been out in years. She left the partying to the younger crowd years ago.

"Girl, I don't even got nothing to wear to even be thinking about taking my old ass to nobody's club." Shelia waved her off.

"Don't even worry about that because after we drop the kids off at Uncle Slim's, we are going to go to the mall, and I am going to buy both of us the fliest fits possible so we can outshine all them hood rats in the building." Fuzzy laughed, making Shelia do the same. Once Shelia realized Fuzzy wasn't giving up and that she had run out of excuses, she gave in. After telling the waitress she was going to be leaving early and putting her in charge as a manager in her absence, Shelia and Fuzzy gathered the kids and were on their way.

"So where are we headed to now?" asked Shelia when Fuzzy got on Hwy 301 heading south.

"To get hairdos," Fuzzy answered, bobbing her head to the latest Nicki Minaj song on the radio." My treat," she added before Shelia could say a word. Shelia slid her designer shades over her eyes, laid her seat back, and enjoyed the ride.

"G.U. Kutts & Styles," Shelia read the letters on the front glass in big bold letters. She'd never been to the salon before but had heard so much about the beautician that owned the place and couldn't wait to see what all the talk was about.

"Ericaaaaa," Fuzzy cheered when she entered the establishment and saw her longtime friend. When Erica looked up from her client's head to see who had entered the shop, she had to do a double take to make sure her eyes weren't playing tricks on her. Erica let out a screeching squeal before she ran over to her friend and held her in a tight bear hug.

"It's about time you bring your tail back from Georgia to let a real stylist do this head," she claimed when she took a step back and touched Fuzzy's edges. Erica was the only beautician that Fuzzy let style her hair.

"I know, right? I just took my braids out before I got on the road to come back home," Fuzzy replied, running her fingers over her edges as well.

"You better be glad you showed up when you did because I was just finishing up on my last client for the day," Erica announced as she made it back over to her styling chair to finish up." Sherry, this is my crazy friend Fuzzy." Fuzzy introduced Shelia to everyone. "So how long are you in town for this time?"

"For the entire summer," Fuzzy admitted.

"Where's those spoiled niece and nephews of mine?" Erica asked, but before Fuzzy got the chance to answer, Erica spoke." Let me guess, with Uncle Slim." They both looked at each other and burst out into laughter." I should've known. Uncle Slim spoils all of his nieces and nephews." They reminisced on when they were coming up until the sound of the bell above the door began to sound, indicating that someone had just entered the building.

"What's up, Cuzo? You about finished with my wife yet?" Hadji asked as he made his way beside her styling chair to get a good look at his wife. When Erica turned and looked in his direction, all he could do was smile. Thoughts of meeting Sherry in that very same shop, sitting in that same exact chair, crossed his mind.

"I'm finishing up now." Hadji took a seat across from them and picked up a GQ magazine after greeting everyone else. Fuzzy, never being the one to forget a face, remembered Hadji from club Drama the night Speedy got killed. She wanted to pull his coattail about the guy Speedy called" Gee" that he was with that night, but figured that now wasn't the time or place to speak on it, so she let it go.

Fifteen minutes later, Erica was handing Sherry a hand-held mirror she could look into so she could see the back of her hair in the huge mirror that hung on the wall behind her." I love it," she admitted, then looked over at Hadji for his approval. He looked up and then sat the magazine down and placed his pointer and thumb finger under his chin in deep thought.

"It's a'ight," he concluded, followed by a big smile. Erica smiled because she loved to see her cousin and Sherry interact with each other. She could feel their love for each other as soon as they entered a room.

"We're gonna see who's grinning when you sleep on the couch tonight," Sherry shot back with an even wider smile on her face. Sherry thanked Erica for her do then headed for the exit.

"Baby, you know I was just joking," Hadji called out then followed behind her out the door.

"Those two are something else," Erica claimed as she waved Fuzzy over to take a seat in her styling chair. Hadji and Sherry interacting with each other reminded Fuzzy of just how much she missed Speedy.

"So what do he do for a living?" Fuzzy asked Erica when she saw Hadji pull off in his canary-yellow Acura NSX.

"He used to hustle, but he got out of the game a while back, right before he got married." Fuzzy's thoughts went back to her late husband and wondered what their lives would have been like if they had chosen to get out of the game earlier and live a normal life. She and Erica chatted about random things until her hair was finished>

"You like?" Erica asked once she finished styling

Fuzzy's hair.

"I love it," she admitted once she looked in the mirror. It only took an hour for Shelia to get her braids put in a style, and they were ready to head to Fuzzy's house to get dressed." You coming out to the old-school jamboree tonight?" she asked Erica after paying for her and Shelia's hairdo.

"Of course I'll be there. I wouldn't dare miss the biggest event of the year. Besides, I got this dope-ass Troop outfit that I got when me and Reese went to New York last year that I've been dying to wear." They all shared a laugh together then headed out the door to go get their nails and feet done for the celebration later on that night.

Fuzzy looked into the full-length mirror on the wall beside her closet door and admired how the throwback black and red Diadora suit snuggly fit her frame like a glove. She glanced at her feet and held them to the side to get a better view of the matching sneakers she had on, then smiled." Damn what am I missing?" she wondered, and then it hit her. Fuzzy made her way around the bed to the walk-in closet on Speedy's side of the bedroom. Once she reached the back, she bent down and put in the code to the safe on the floor." Now I'm complete," Fuzzy answered her own question then rubbed her fingers over the 40" dookie rope that Speedy always sported to the event. She completed the fit with her four-finger ring with the word" FUZZ" across the front of it.

KNOCK, KNOCK, KNOCK

"Come in," Fuzzy called out, then made her way back into her bedroom." You look beautiful," she said in awe when she spotted Shelia standing in the doorway, striking a model's pose. Even though Shelia was knocking on fifty years old, her thick and curvaceous figure filled out her all-black 8-ball body dress perfectly. It left very little for the imagination.

"I can't believe that I let you talk me into going out tonight," Shelia admitted, making her way over to Fuzzy's full-length mirror to get a better look at her outfit. She had to admit that ever since she had return from rehab, she had been feeling a lot better about herself.

"Anyway," Fuzzy waved her off." I hope I look half as good as you do when I reach your age. If I do, them young girls better watch out," Fuzzy joked, then made her way to the nightstand on the other side of the room to get her cell off the charger.

Once they made sure they were as fly as they

could be, they headed downstairs into the kitchen which led to the five-car garage, or the "show room" as Speedy used to call it, to pick out which car that they were going to drive to the club. "Take your pick." Fuzzy gestured to the variety of vehicles. Shelia's eyes went from the all-black Rubicon Jeep that Speedy used to ride out in when he did his dirt, to the drophead coupe that he bought Fuzzy for an anniversary gift, on down to Fuzzy's four-door Maybach. Shelia looked to the next car and was about to pick Speedy's S550 until her eyes stopped on the two-door Maybach coupe. Fuzzy smiled on the inside when she saw the look in Shelia's eyes. "The Bat Mobile it is." Fuzzy cheered then grabbed the key fob out of the key cabinet hanging on the wall. Once they were situated in the coupe, Fuzzy hit the "start" button, and the engine came to life. Even though it had been a year since the car had been started, it still purred like a baby kitten. "I'ma stunt for you tonight, baby," she whispered to Speedy when the garage door slid upward. Fuzzy and Shelia were about to make it a night that the city of Wilson was never going to forget.

All eyes were on the white-on-white Maybach coupe when Fuzzy and Shelia pulled up in front of the red carpet at club Drama. So many memories of the night of Speedy's untimely demise rushed into Fuzzy's mind as she sat behind the wheel and stared at the front door entrance.

"You sure you're ready for this?" Shelia asked after noticing the worried look that was written all over Fuzzy's face. Instead of responding, Fuzzy pulled down the sun visor, took the pair of Cazal's from it, and then slid them over her eyes.

"Come on, let's do this." When Fuzzy tossed the driver's door in the air, the valet was there with his hand out to accept the key fob and give Fuzzy her ticket. By the time she retrieved her ticket and walked around the car, Shelia was waiting for her at the beginning of the red carpet so they could make their grand entrance. The paparazzi's and bystanders' camera lights flashed at a hundred miles per hour trying to get pictures of the two as they made their way to the entrance. Being that Fuzzy now stayed in Atlanta and Shelia never went out to any of the clubs, everyone wondered who the two stallions could be.

"I need to see your Elite Passes please," the big, burly looking bouncer at the entrance announced when Fuzzy and Shelia made it to the front. After looking Shelia up and down, he directed his attention toward Fuzzy. That's when he realized who she was. "Oh shiittt! Where have you been?" he asked, then gave her a big brotherly hug. Fuzzy smiled and returned the hug. She remembered the day Speedy first hired the big man that she came to know as "Big Bear."

"You know me, Bear; I've been around." After promising to get at him before she left to go back to Atlanta, he let them in without bothering to search either of their purses. When they entered the club, Fuzzy realized that more people had decided to show than she had anticipated. As she made her way through the club she noticed that a lot of things had been redecorated and the thing that caught her attention the most was the background drop of the picture area. She stood frozen as she stared at the life-size painting of the picture she took of Speedy and Menace the day they picked Menace up from rehab and threw him a party at Big Mama's Kitchen. She made a mental note to take a picture and find out who the artist was that drew the picture so she could pay him to paint a portrait of her and Speedy that they took together when they went to Morehead Beach for the spring festival. "Oh shit, the queen is here," DJ Ollie B called out over the microphone. The guy controlling the spotlight found who the DJ was talking about and planted the spotlight on Fuzzy. She played it off even though the light had caught her off guard. "This is for you, big sis." A second later followed by a few scratches from the DJ, the hit single "Ladies First" by Queen Latifah blasted through the speakers. The crowd went crazy and started waving their arms from side to side as they sung along with the lyrics. That was Fuzzy's and Shelia's cue to make their escape to the bar and out of the spotlight.

"Let us get two bottles of Moscato," Fuzzy ordered, then placed her back against the bar and looked out at the sea of people. Shelia was about to speak, until a familiar voice caught both of their attention.

"How in the hell did you get her to come out?" Lil Man questioned Fuzzy with a raised eyebrow. He and the rest of the crew had been trying for years to get Shelia to come party with them, but she would always decline. Lil Man shook his head then gave them both a hug just as the barmaid had returned with their bottles.

"That'll be $200," she informed with a hint of an attitude. Kia was a new barmaid that Lil Man had given the pleasure of letting her top him off a few times. Even though she had wanted more, Lil Man kept her in her place. Fuzzy was about to hand the barmaid the money, but Lil Man intervened.

"They're with me," he announced with a smirk on his face then took the bottles and handed them to Fuzzy and Shelia. After placing his arms around their shoulders, Lil Man led them to the elevator so they could go up to the second floor with the elite ballers and have some real fun.

As soon as they stepped into the elite VIP section of the club, the entire atmosphere changed. There was no longer the smell of cheap cologne or perfume, or the sight of so-called players wearing fake jewelry or knock-off outfits. All you could smell and see from wall to wall was money. Not in the sense of greenbacks, but the people that represented royalty, and their guests, of course. "Is my eyes playing tricks on me?" Tank strained his eyes when he spotted Fuzzy and Shelia in the place. "Because I know that ain't Shelia who I see up in this bitch!" Tank joked as he made his way across the room to greet his partner. After giving Shelia a hug, he made his way to Fuzzy and saluted her.

"Whatever, boy." She waved him off and hugged

his neck. "You better give your big sister a hug. Both Lil Man and Tank had become close to Fuzzy, and she considered them like little brothers to her. They had proven their loyalty to her on plenty of occasions. After their short embrace Tank stepped back and let her have it. "I thought that me and Lil Man had to take a trip to the 'A' and make sure nobody ain't kidnapped you and the kids." Tank laughed.

"Boy, please. You must forget who you talking to," Fuzzy responded. Tank placed both of his hands in the air in surrender and took another step back. Even though he had never personally witnessed Fuzzy put in any work, her name certainly rang bells in the streets.

"Come on, y'all," Lil Man cut in and motioned for everyone to follow him to the vacant VIP booth in the far corner. That was his and Tank's personal booth. They chose it because they didn't like sitting with their back to the entrance, also because it gave them a clear view of everyone from every angle in the room.

They sat in the booth laughing, drinking, and enjoying themselves until one of Shelia's favorite old-school songs blasted through the speakers. "Come on, girl," Shelia squealed, then grabbed Fuzzy by the hand and pulled her to the dance floor. Fuzzy danced in awe as she watched Shelia do her thing. She couldn't believe how up-to-date Shelia's dance moves were.

Three songs and a couple of sweats later, Fuzzy's buzz started to kick in and she began to get winded, so it was a relief to her when a handsome, older-looking gentleman asked her to cut in and dance with Shelia. Once Shelia assured Fuzzy that she would be okay, Fuzzy made her way back to the booth, where she spotted Slim sitting in her seat, across the table from Lil Man, with his two bodyguards on each side.

"Fuzzy," Slim stood and greeted his only niece. "I thought you said Shelia was coming out with you," he mentioned when he noticed her come up alone.

"She did. She's out on the dance floor doing her

CONNECTED TO THE PLUG 3

thang." Fuzzy pointed. Slim looked out to the dancefloor and spotted Shelia putting it on an older-looking guy. Slim's mind reflected back to when Shelia was once the baddest woman in the city, when the two were an item. Long before she got on drugs and caught HIV. Slim was brought back to the present by the sound of Tank commenting on two beautiful women at the bar by themselves. Slim looked toward the bar area and smiled when he realized who Tank was referring to.

"Excuse me." Lil Man and Tank stood amazed by Slim's side as he waved the two Brazilian twins over to join them. "Ladies, these are my two nephews, Lil Man and Tank," Slim introduced. The twins smiled and waved as they stared with opened mouths." And I'm sure you two remember my niece." The twins looked over at Fuzzy surprised.

"Hey, Fuzzy. Long time no see," the twins greeted her in unison. Fuzzy had no idea that the twins were still dealing with her uncle after all the years that had passed since Speedy had told her to go get the twins for her uncle in the same exact club, on the same exact night. They listened as Slim told a few jokes, as usual, before he ended up calling it a night. As soon as Slim and the twins got on the elevator, all hell broke loose.

"Shelia," Fuzzy instantly thought to herself. Without giving it a second thought, she raced through the crowd, pushing and shoving until she made it to the middle of the dancefloor. "What happened?" Fuzzy asked as Shelia stood over the older gentleman who lay in the fetal position at her feet.

"This chump just couldn't take no for an answer and kept trying to reach under my dress." Lil Man and Tank waved two big bouncers over, instructing them to take him out of the back exit of the club. That was the cue to get rid of the guy, for good. They wanted to send a clear message that if anybody messed with the family, they would get dealt with accordingly.

At two o'clock, Fuzzy and Shelia decided to call

it a night. Lil Man noticed Fuzzy sway to the side when she stood to her feet. "Oh hell naw," he jumped to his feet with his hand out. "Let me get that ticket." Fuzzy looked into his eyes to see if he was serious.

"Boy, I'm good." She waved him off when she saw that he was.

"Yeah right. Ain't no way I'm letting you drive home from here. Besides, if anything happened to you under my watch, Slim would have my ass." Fuzzy knew Lil Man was telling the truth, so when she fished the ticket from her purse, she reluctantly handed it over to him.

When they made it outside, to Fuzzy's surprise, the "Bat Mobile" was already out front waiting on them with the engine running and Big Bear guarding it with his life. Since the two-door Maybach only seated two people, Fuzzy hopped in the passenger's seat, and Shelia jumped in Tank's Audi R8 with him.

Lil Man led the way to Fuzzy's place and informed Fuzzy that he would call her later on in the week with the money he owed. Also, since business had picked up over the past months, he would be wanting to step the order up. Fuzzy was very proud of Lil Man and the decision she made to put him in charge once Speedy died.

After Lil Man and Tank made sure Fuzzy and Shelia were safe inside, they headed back to the club to see what they could get into before the night was over. Shelia stayed up most of the night telling Fuzzy stories of Speedy and Menace until they cried then laughed themselves to sleep.

The first place Lil Man headed when they got back to the club was the bar. Tank, on the other hand, headed straight to the restroom to relieve himself. "Let me get a bottle of Moet," he ordered, then turned around to look out into the crowded room of partygoers. He smiled to himself thinking how proud his mentor, Speedy, would have been of him if he could see him now. His thoughts were interrupted by the loud slam of his bottle hitting the bar top. When he turned around, he was met by a venomous stare from Kia. "I know you didn't try to play me in front of that bitch up in here earlier," she barked, snaking her neck and pointing her finger. A few patrons turned their attention to the couple, waiting for an altercation to pop off.

"Who the fuck you think you talking too?" Lil Man snapped through slitted eyes. Kia saw the death in Lil Man's eyes and toned it down a notch.

"Why are you doing me like this?" Lil Man calmed down a little when he saw the tears welling up in Kia's eyes. Even though he was a killer at heart, there was something about a woman in tears that did something to him. Although this was a decision he knew he would regret in the future, he summoned her to his office in the back. Hearing that, Kia's mood brightened quicker than a New York minute. On Lil Man's way back to his office, he ran into Tank coming out of the restroom.

"Yo, where you on your way to? The party's back that away," he said, pointing back to the dancefloor. Just as Lil Man was about to answer, Kia came beside him and wrapped her arm around his waist.

"Come on, daddy," she pleaded while licking her lips. Tank looked from Lil Man to Kia then back to Lil Man.

"You wilding, homie," Tank admitted, thinking about how Meka would react if she got word from one of her many friends that were in the club. Before Lil Man got the chance to respond, Kia was pulling him down the hallway.

As soon as they stepped into Lil Man's office, Kia was all over him. "You know we can't keep doing this right?"

"Uh huh," Kia agreed as she went down on both knees and unfastened his belt. She knew what she was doing was wrong but she figured what her cousin didn't know wouldn't hurt her. Truth be told, Kia had been jealous of Meka since they were kids. She claimed that Meka always had the best of everything. The best parents, the best clothes, and most of all, the best men when it came down to relationships. This time, she wanted to win too. That's why when Meka made the fatal mistake and asked Lil Man to hire her cousin since she needed a job, Kia took full advantage of the opportunity. Even though giving him head was as far as Lil Man would allow things to go, Kia was cool with that because she knew if Meka ever slipped up, she would be there to catch him.

"Shit," Lil Man cursed as he released his heavy load down her throat. Kia looked up with him still in her mouth and moaned. "You gotta stop acting up in public," he warned her.

"I know, daddy. You forgive me?" Kia pouted then licked her lips, making sure Lil Man's kids all went in her mouth. Kia tried to lean in for a kiss, but Lil Man quickly dodged to his left and headed to the bathroom to get himself back together before the headed back to the club area. When he returned, he handed her a handful of money.

"I'm good, daddy," she declined. It wasn't that she didn't want it. She was looking at the long run and knew that things would be greater in the future once she captured his heart. At least that's what she hoped for.

The first person Tank saw in VIP was one of his brother's longtime friends. "Yo, Hadji, what it do, big homie?"

Hadji stood up and turned his attention to the voice behind him. "What's good, Tank?" Hadji responded then dapped him up. "How's it been going?" Hadji was glad to see that Tank was doing good for himself after his older brother was gunned down a few years ago. Word was that his side chick set him up to get robbed one night when they were coming out of the hotel room. Being that he wasn't willing to come up off of his money, the stick-up kid shot and killed him. When word got back to Tank of what the chick did, he put a bullet in the middle of her heart and knocked it out of her chest. Now she was really heartless.

"Everything's good on my end. How about you?"

"You know me, taking it one day at a time."

Tank was about to ask him about getting back in the game, but before he got the chance to speak on it, a slim, sexy chocolate thang caught his attention at the other end of the bar. Hadji retired from the game when he met his wife, Sherry, and vowed to her that he wouldn't indulge in any more illegal activity. He'd been able to keep his promise so far.

"Big homie, I'ma get up with you later. Duty calls," Tank laughed then made his way down the bar to the slim chocolate female at the end. "Is this seat taken?" Tank asked as he took the seat beside her.

"It is now." Chocolate looked to Tank then answered.

"So what you drinking?" After telling Tank what she was sipping on, he ordered her an entire bottle.

"Big baller, huh?" Chocolate smiled.

"I just think fine women should have the finer things in life," Tank replied honestly.

"Is that right?" Chocolate smiled. "Well why are we at the bar instead of over there?" She pointed over at the elite VIP section.

"We're not. You are," Tank joked and made his way over to his special VIP booth. Even though Tank never looked back to see if Chocolate was following, he knew she was. After the bouncer allowed him entrance, Tank took a seat and popped the cork on the bottle of champagne. Once the suds ran over, he took it straight to the head. "She's with me," he told the bouncer that had Chocolate hemmed up at the rope entrance. "What took you so long?" Tank smiled when Chocolate took the seat beside him.

"I think if you would have told me your name, it would have been easier to get in," Chocolate answered, then rolled her eyes.

"Oh, now we giving names, because if my memory serves me well, you didn't give me your name either." Through all of the flirting that was going on, Chocolate had forgotten that she didn't give Tank her name.

"You can call me Sina."

Tank took her hand in his then kissed the back of it. "Nice to meet you. You can call me Tank." Sina stared at Tank for a minute like she was star struck. She had heard about Tank through a few friends, but to be up close and personal was unreal. She knew she had to make a good impression if she wanted to be on his arm. After ten minutes of getting to know each other, Tank was escorting her out of VIP to the elevator.

Before they made it out of the club, Tank ran into Lil Man and Kia.

"I'm about to be out, bruh," Tank announced, then dapped his partner up. After their short embrace, Tank looked at Kia in disgust. Right then and there he made it his business to stay as far away as possible from her. In his eyes Kia was nothing but poison. If she could cross her own cousin, there was no telling what she would do to an outsider. Lil Man watched Tank and the chocolate slim chick on his arm make their way out front where Tank's Audi R8 waited on them.

3

Lil Man followed his baby mamma, Meka, through the mall, with an arm full of shopping bags, as she pushed Lil Lucky in his baby stroller. Even though Lil Man loved her to death, he was reminded why he hated to go with her shopping. This would make their second trip to the truck to put her bags away. That was the least he could do since she was there for him when he was on the come-up and gave him the most important thing anyone could ever give him, his son, which he named after his cousin, Lucky.

On their way through the parking lot, Lil Man's cell began to ring. "What?" he snapped into the phone without looking at the display screen. Meka fished her keys out of her handbag and hit the trunk button so Lil Man could put the bags away. "How bad is it?" A few seconds later Meka heard Lil Man tell the caller that he would be there in fifteen minutes. Then he ended the call. By the time he made it to the side of Meka's truck, she was opening the back door to the Range Rover Sport to place Lil Lucky into his car seat. She found herself face-to-face with Lil Man when she finished. Before Lil Man could apologize she placed a finger to his lips. "Oh yeah, nigga. You most definitely owe me one for this." She smiled then made her way around him and hoped behind the wheel and started the engine. Lil Man shook his head from side to side then made his way around to the passenger's side. He then told Meka the destination he needed her to take him to.

Once Meka pulled up in front of club Drama, Lil Man leaned over and kissed her on the lips. "I'll get Tank to bring me home when I'm done here," he informed her, then reached for the door handle. When he opened the door, Meka cleared her throat to get his attention.

"I didn't finish shopping," she reminded him with her hand out. Lil Man pulled the stack out of his right pocket and handed it over to her. "Oh yeah, we need to eat too," she joked once she placed the money in her handbag.

"I'll see y'all when I get home." Lil Man smiled then looked into the backseat at Lil Lucky, who had fallen asleep on the way over to the club.

"When we leave the mall I'm going to take Lil Lucky by my mom's house. She keeps complaining that she don't see her only grandson enough." Meka shook her head in disbelief since she kept him every other weekend. After blowing Meka a kiss, Lil Man headed into the club to handle his business.

"Over there." Tank flagged his partner over to the bar where he and a crew member that went by the name of Jamontae were indulging in a bottle of Hennessy. Once Lil Man fixed a stiff drink as well, he waited for someone to tell him the important reason why he had to cut his family day to attend the meeting. "You remember last week when I told you that one of our spots on the North Side was coming up short with our money," Tank reminded Lil Man. "Well, word is that this Jersey Crew popped out of nowhere and set up shop around the corner from ours with some high-powered shit." Lil Man took a sip from his shot glass and pondered over the situation at hand. He knew that he had to think before he made a move, because if this new crew had the product to slow their money down, they had to be dealing with someone much higher up the ladder with a lot of power.

"Do anyone know the name of the cat that's backing them?" Lil Man questioned as he refilled his glass.

"One of my loyal customers said that he overheard some friends of his say that they heard one of the Jersey cats mention the name B.B. or some shit like that," Jamontae answered. Lil Man repeated the name over and over in his head, hoping to come up with a face to it, but came up blank. That only infuriated him even more. After downing one last glass full of Henny, Lil Man slammed the glass on the bar top then demanded that Jamontae get some answers, and fast. Jamontae whipped out his cell on his way out of the club with hopes of finding out who was behind the Jersey Crew. He knew if he did, he would get a huge promotion up the food chain in their crew, and that's exactly what he planned to do.

$ $ $

Lil Man, Tank, and Jamontae, along with five more crew members, all filed out of the back of the club and hopped into two black work vans that waited outside for them. Lil Man was determined now more than ever to find out who the Jersey kid named B.B. was, by any means necessary.

The two vans parked a block down from the Jersey Crew's trap house. They watched patiently as traffic came and went like clockwork. This just added more fuel to the already burning fire in Lil Man. There was nothing that he hated more than money being taken from him or his family. That was definitely a no-no. "Aye, ain't that that faggot-ass Luke coming outta the spot?" Jamontae asked from the passenger seat, squinting his eyes trying to get a better look.

"Hell yeah, that's that nigga," Diontae confirmed as Luke approached the van they sat in. Luke was so much in a hurry to cut between the two abandoned houses a few steps away, he didn't even notice the side door to one of the black vans slide open until two masked men snatched him inside.

"Yo, what's dis about?" Luke slurred between his two missing front teeth. Luke had snatched so many purses, broken into so many houses, and worst of all, snatched so many drug dealers' packs, he didn't know, which was the reason that landed him in such a tight situation.

"Where's my money, muthafucka?" Jamontae barked, pressing the Mac-11 in his hand to the side of Luke's head. After hearing Jamontae's menacing voice, Luke knew he had some hell-of-a explaining to do if he wanted to make it out of the back of the van with his life. Ever since his girlfriend introduced him to the Jersey Boyz' product, every dime he made, found, or stole went straight to them. It seemed like the most logical thing to do at the time, but now Luke was regretting his decision. Just as Jamontae cocked his gun arm back to smack Luke upside his head, Lil Man stopped him.

"Hold up." A thought flashed through his head and he planned to use it to their advantage. "Look, as you can see, it's not looking good for you, my boy," he began, then looked from Luke to Jamontae. "You must owe my man a lot of loot the way he acting."

"It ain't nothing but two hundred dollars," Luke cleared up.

"Three hundred dollars now, bitch," Jamontae interrupted before kicking Luke in his stomach. Luke cried out in pain as he balled up in the fetal position on the van's floor. Before Jamontae could deliver another kick, Lil Man intervened.

"This is what I'm going to do for you, Luke." Lil

Man paused then went into his pants pocket and pulled out a wad of cash. Luke's eyes lit up as Lil Man peeled five one hundred dollar bills off the stack of money then held it out to him. Just as Luke reached his hand out to accept them, Lil Man pulled them back.

"All of this can be yours, IF you go back to the Jersey Boyz' trap house and cop some more crack." Luke knew that what he was about to do was a death wish because he had seen first-hand what the Jersey Boyz were capable of a few weeks ago when a fiend tried their hand and ran off with one of their packs. But at the time he had no other choice. He was damned if he did, and he would be damned if he didn't. Luke sat for a few more seconds and weighed out his options.

"Fuck it. I'll do it," he decided, then snatched the money out of Lil Man's hand before Lil Man changed his mind and made him do it for free anyway. Once Lil Man gave Luke exact instructions, he opened the side door to the van for Luke to make his exit. "What?" Luke asked Jamontae as he blocked his exit.

"What my ass, nigga. Let me get that." Luke took off three one-hundred-dollar bills and reluctantly handed them over to Jamontae. "Nice doing business with you." Jamontae smiled as he placed the money in his pocket. The first thing Luke thought about when his feet hit the pavement was to take off running through the cut with the little crack he had in his pocket and the two hundred dollars he had left over from the money Lil Man gave him. The flicking light from the cigarette being lit in the van behind the one he just got out off made him erase that thought from his mind. Luke was fast, but he doubted if he could outrun two vans full of killers.

Lil Man and the crew watched Luke enter the trap house before they made their move. The two vans crept up the block at a snail's pace before parking in front of the trap house. Each crew member took up their post, and as soon as the door came open, Tank yoked up the first member of the Jersey Crew then forced his way inside. By the time the second Jersey Crew member knew what was going on, he was knocked out cold by Jamontae's Mac-11. The third and final Jersey Boy was about to press his luck and reach for the sawed-off under the cushion of the couch that he was sitting on, but Diontae's 9 mm pressing against the side of his head made him think twice about it. "Make my day, pussy," Diontae threatened through gritted teeth at the same time Lil Man entered the room. Jamontae yoked up Luke just to make things look good.

"Where's B.B.?" Lil Man questioned the third crew member.

"I ain't telling y'all country-ass niggas shit," he laughed. "Get the fuck outta here!" he waved them off. Those were the last words he spoke before Lil Man sent a slug to the middle of his forehead.

"I hope you're smarter than your friend here," Lil Man stated after turning to the Jersey Boy Tank had yoked up.

"Fuck you, nigga. When B.B. gets word of this

you're all dead," the Jersey Boy promised. Tank, not the one to take threats lightly, began to apply pressure to the yoke hold he had the Jersey Boy in. He didn't realize how strong the hold was until his body went limp.

"My fault," Tank apologized then released his grip. When the dead body hit the floor, Lil Man walked over the second Jersey Boy and smacked him across his face.

"What happened?" he questioned, looking around for his partners. It finally hit him when he saw their dead bodies sprawled out on the floor.

"Are you going to be the smart one and talk, or are you going to end up like the rest of these fools?" Lil Man asked him.

The Jersey Boy looked at all the dead bodies around him, and decided to do what Lil Man wanted. "A'ight, I'll call him." He took out his phone and scrolled through the contacts. After he chose B.B. and clicked send, they all listened over speakerphone as the phone rang twice and then was picked up.

"Yeah."

"Hey, boss, I got someone here who wants to talk to you."

"Who is it, and it better not be some no-name underling."

"Underling? I'll show you an underling. Open your mouth." After doing as he was told, Lil Man placed his gun inside then blew the back of the Jersey Boy's head out. "Do this underling got your attention now?" Lil Man said toward the phone still in the Jersey Boy's hand, with a smirk on his face.

"All you did was save me a bullet, because I was definitely going to kill that coward when I saw him for even calling my phone for you. I guess now I'll just kill his mother. But before I do that 'LIL MAN,' I'm going to kill you first." Lil Man looked around the room, wondering how the caller knew who he was. "Now that I got your undivided attention," B.B. stated." I will be seeing you real soon to finish our unfinished business." Before Lil Man could say a word, the line went dead.

"Let's go," Lil Man ordered. Before they walked out of the trap house, Jamontae turned Luke around and looked into his eyes.

"Yo, I ain't seen shit," Luke claimed right before Jamontae sent a slug between his eyes.

"I never liked your punk ass anyway," he admitted, then ran Luke's pockets for the rest of the money he had on him.

$ $ $

A few days went by, and Lil Man still had no idea who this B.B. character was or how he knew who he was. There was one thing he was certain of, and that was that him and his entire crew had to be on their p's and q's if they planned to make it through another day.

$ $ $

"Is everything alright, baby?" Stacy asked when B.B. ended the call.

"Things couldn't be better," B.B. answered

honestly, then dove headfirst back into Stacy's love nest.

"Oh baby," she whispered in pleasure, running her manicured fingernails through B.B.'s neatly twisted locks. For the past few weeks that B.B. had relocated back to Wilson from New Jersey, Stacy hadn't left her house, besides going to the beauty salon or the nail shop to get prepped up, and that's exactly how B.B. wanted it.

After bringing Stacy to another orgasm, B.B. slid out of bed and went to the shower to clean up then hit the streets to check up on a few things.

$ $ $

Fuzzy had just put the kids to sleep and was about to climb in bed herself, when she heard her cell phone go off. "Hello," she answered on the third ring.

"We might have a problem," the caller announced. Fuzzy let out a long sigh then walked across the room and sat in Speedy's favorite recliner and waited for Lil Man to fill her in on the problem.

"It was brought to my attention earlier by one of our crew members that someone had set up shop on our territory," he began, then filled her in on how they went to their spot and wreaked havoc on the Jersey Boyz Crew.

"Did we lose any of ours?" Fuzzy asked, concerned.

"Nah, but the strange part of it all, the head nigga named B.B. called me by my name like he knew we were coming. Fuzzy thought for a few seconds about what Lil Man said, and found it odd indeed.

"I'll call Uncle Slim and have him look into this B.B. character and get back with you." After discussing the re-up plan for the following day, Fuzzy ended the call and phoned Slim.

"Baby girl, to what do I owe the pleasure of this call?" Slim smiled into the phone, always loving to hear from his only niece. His smile slowly faded as Fuzzy relayed the news that Lil Man laid on her just moments earlier. Before Fuzzy ended the call, she had one more question for Slim.

"Do you know this guy by the name of Hadji?" Slim sat quietly on the phone thinking of the protégé his brother, Mr. Biggs, had plans to pass the torch down to before he died. Once Slim explained to Fuzzy how he knew of Hadji, he promised to set up a meeting with them then ended the call. Fuzzy put her phone on the charger then climbed in bed. She thought of the mysterious guy named Hadji. She hated to admit it, but there was something about him that plagued her interest though she couldn't quite put a finger on it. Maybe it was because her father had interest in him, or maybe it was because he reminded her so much of her late husband. Whatever it was, she was going to find out sooner or later. She just hoped it would be sooner.

4

❝So what's the word?" B.B. asked Joe when he slid into the passenger seat of B.B.'s Maserati. Joe was B.B.'s younger brother. He talked B.B. into returning to Wilson to set up shop in their old North Side neighborhood. There was too much money being made, and Joe wanted in on it. B.B. was against it at first, but once Joe promised to deliver Lil Man's head on a silver platter, B.B. caught the first plane back home.

"My girl told me she just came from getting her hair done at a salon called Above and Beyond, and guess who she saw?" Joe looked at B.B. as if he was waiting on a response. After realizing that B.B. wasn't in a guessing mood, Joe answered his own question. "Meka, Lil Man's baby mama!" B.B.'s eyes lit up and a smile appeared.

"Go on," B.B. encouraged, pressing to hear the information that Joe had in store.

"My girl said that she overheard Meka saying that her and Lil Man were going to drop their son off at her mother's place and then go out to eat tonight." That news was like music to B.B.'s ears.

"Where at?" B.B. asked, then looked over into Joe's eyes. Joe looked off into space, trying to remember the name of the restaurant. "It was called Big Mama's Kitchen," Joe put up a finger and shouted out.

B.B. sat back and looked out of the front windshield, trying to remember the location of the place. "Big Mama's, Big Mama's," and then it came clear. "Fuzzy's old restaurant," B.B. said out loud. B.B. wanted Fuzzy dead just as bad as he wanted Lil Man dead, if not worse. They had a score to settle, and B.B. was going to settle it in blood. B.B. leaned over, reached into the glove compartment, and pulled out a brown paper bag. After inspecting the contents inside, Joe placed it in his coat pocket and grabbed the door handle. "I'll hit you in a couple of days to check on you," B.B. told Joe before he made his exit.

Before Joe disappeared into his trap house he looked back and gave B.B. a salute. After saluting back, B.B. pulled out into traffic and headed back to Stacy's place. On the way, all B.B. could think about was Fuzzy. They had a lot of history, and B.B. couldn't wait to return the favor and make her life a living hell. "You're gonna wish you never heard of me, bitch," B.B. promised, then let the sounds of the old school classic "The Big Payback" by EPMD blast through the speakers.

$ $ $

When B.B. entered the house, Stacy immediately sensed that something was wrong. "Get dressed," B.B. ordered, then headed to the walk-in closet to find an outfit to wear out to dinner for the night. Stacy knew better than to ask questions when B.B. gave orders, so she made her way into the closet to do as she was told.

Satisfied with her outfit. Stacy joined B.B. in the bathroom to freshen up. Once they were dressed, B.B. checked the clip to the P89 to make sure it was full to the tip, and then led Stacy out of the house and hopped in the all-black SRT-8 Dodge Charger.

Soon after, they were pulling into Big Mama's Kitchen.

"I've always wanted to eat here," Stacy admitted. "I heard they got the best soul food in town." B.B. looked at Stacy in disgust. If Stacy knew how close she was to getting slapped across her face, she would've kept her comments to herself. B.B. pulled into a parking spot between a red Jaguar and a gray Panamera, then made their way into the elegant restaurant.

"This shit is nice," B.B. whispered as the hostess led the way to their table where they ordered their meal. Ten minutes later B.B. noticed two suspicious looking guys dressed in all black enter the restaurant. B.B. wouldn't have given it much thought, but they sat at two different tables and began looking around for anything out of the ordinary.

"Thank you," Stacy told the waitress after she placed their dinner onto the table. Just as they were about to take their first bite, the couple of the hour entered, looking like a million bucks. B.B. had to admit, the female that Lil Man was sporting on his arm was one of the sexiest chicks in the building.

After pulling the Yankees fitted down low, B.B. looked away from the couple and started eating. B.B. peeped up just as Shelia approached Lil Man's table. B.B. had almost forgotten about Shelia. Watching her nod at the two guys dressed in black, B.B.'s suspicions were confirmed.

B.B. watched and plotted from a distance as Lil Man and his baby mama laughed and talked over dinner. By the time the couple had finished, B.B. had come up with a master plan to destroy Lil Man and Fuzzy's life. B.B. ran down the plan to Stacy on their way home.

"My cousin Sawanda would be perfect for this job," she suggested.

B.B. didn't know Stacy's cousin personally, but had heard of a lot of grimy things that she had done to get paid in the past and figured she could get the job done with no problem. After Stacy called Sawanda up and ran down the scheme to her, the only question Sawanda had was when and how much would she get paid.

A month had passed since B.B. paid Stacy's cousin Sawanda half for applying to be a third shift manager at Big Mama's Kitchen. Just when B.B. was about to give up on all hope, Stacy rushed into the bedroom and handed him her cell phone. "A lady named Ms. Shelia just called and informed me that I just got the job if I still wanted it," Sawanda cheered into the receiver. That was like music to B.B.'s ears. "She said I could come in later on today so she can show me the ropes and if I liked the job, it was mine." B.B. looked at the calendar that hung on the wall.

"Thirty days," B.B. said out loud, estimating the time it would probably take to complete mission. After ending the call, B.B. turned to a smiling Stacy and handed her a brown envelope. "Go take this to Sawanda and tell her the rest will come when she do what we planned out." Stacy took the envelope and headed out the door to do what she was told to do.

$ $ $

When Shelia walked into her office, the first thing she did was kick off her shoes and sit in the recliner behind her desk. She smiled to herself, happy to finally be off of her feet. "Umm," she moaned out loud, rubbing her aching toes. She couldn't believe that she had been working for thirteen hours straight, until she looked at her watch a second time. "Damn, it's 11:00 p.m.," she said out loud, not believing that she worked all day without taking a single break. The first thing she planned to do when she walked into her condo was head to the Jacuzzi and soak her aching bones. "Come in," she called out. Sawanda entered the office with a deposit bag filled with receipts and earnings made from the business day and sat them on top of Shelia's desk.

"Boy, we were busy today," Sawanda commented as she watched Shelia go over the receipts. After checking the money count, Shelia finally looked up at Sawanda, impressed. Not only was the money count on point, but she also had all of the receipts in order as well. Not to mention, the month that Sawanda had been working at Big Mama's Kitchen, business had picked up tremendously.

"Yes, we were busy today," Shelia finally responded to Sawanda's earlier comment. "It should be even busier tomorrow," she admitted, since tomorrow was Friday. Shelia stood to her feet and made her way around to the other side of the desk to the coat rack. "You ready to get out of here?" Sawanda and Shelia made small talk until they walked out of the restaurant. "Do you think that you'll be able to come in a little early tomorrow?" Shelia asked after locking up.

"Yep," Sawanda cheered, thinking about the extra hours. Truth be told, she was really feeling her job and started hating the fact that it had to come to an end.

"Good. Is ten o'clock too early?"

"No ma'am. I'll be here at 9:45 a.m.," she assured her boss as she headed to her car. Once Shelia found her key, she reached to put the key in the door. That's when she noticed her front tire was completely flat.

"Shit."

"What's the matter?" Sawanda asked, shutting her car door and rushing over to see what had Shelia cursing.

"If it ain't one thing, it's another," Shelia concluded, pointing down at the flat.

"You don't have to call anyone. I will be glad to take you home, or wherever you need to go," Sawanda assured her. Being that it was so late, Shelia decided to take Sawanda up on her offer instead of bothering Fuzzy to come pick her up. Besides she really didn't want Fuzzy to wake the kids and bring them out of the house at that time of night.

"You sure?"

"Yes, I'm sure. This is the least I can do for you hiring me!" Sawanda waved her off then headed back in the direction of her car.

After making Sawanda take the twenty-dollar bill for gas money, Shelia reminded her to be to work at ten o'clock. "Nine forty-five," Sawanda countered. She watched as Shelia made her way into her condo before she picked up her cell phone to call B.B. Once Sawanda made B.B. repeat Shelia's address twice, she headed home to wait on Stacy to bring the remainder of her money to her.

$ $ $

"You sure she's in there alone?" Joe asked as he stood bent over picking the lock to the back door.

"Yeah, I'm sure, nigga," B.B. answered, looking around for anything out of the ordinary. Fifteen seconds later, Joe was leading the way into the condo. The first room they entered was the kitchen, and then a narrow hallway that led to a set of stairs.

Once they reached the second floor, they could see a light from the television coming from the second bedroom door. B.B. followed Joe's lead, and when they both entered the bedroom, they were like deer stuck in the headlights. Shelia lay across the bed on her stomach with her thick legs peeking from underneath her robe. Even though she was up in age, Shelia's body was still amazing. Snapping out of their lustful thoughts, B.B. and Joe made their way over to the bed. "Wake up, bitch," B.B. barked, then slapped Shelia so hard, when she woke up she saw stars.

"What do y'all want?" Shelia asked once she gained her focus. B.B. and Joe gawked at Shelia's nakedness as she sat up on her knees in the middle of the bed holding the right side of her face. Once Shelia realized what had their attention, she slowly reached for her robe and closed it.

"What's that nigga Lil Man's address?" B.B. asked after the free peep show.

"Who?" Shelia asked, dumbfounded. The only

answer she got to her question was another slap across her face, this time sending her off the bed onto the floor.

"Get that bitch up," B.B. ordered Joe. Joe went over to the other side of the bed, picked Shelia up off the floor by her hair, then got behind her and put her in a tight choke hold. Shelia could feel Joe pressing his erection against her backside." So you wanna play tough, huh?" There was no way Shelia was going to give Lil Man or anyone else in the crew up. She'd rather die.

"No, no, no," she began to plea when B.B. pulled out a bag of heroin and a brand-new syringe.

"I swear I don't know where he stay," she promised with tears in her eyes, but B.B. wasn't convinced. Before Shelia knew what was happening, she was air lifted and slammed to the ground, knocking the wind out of her. She struggled as Joe sat across her chest and pinned her arms down with his knees." Please don't do this," she begged, but her pleas fell on deaf ears. She watched as B.B. loaded the needle with deadly poison. It was enough to knock out a grown horse. Shelia closed her eyes and said a silent prayer as she felt the potent drug flow through her veins. After Shelia's eyes shut, B.B. removed the syringe.

"You know what to do," B.B. ordered, then walked out of the room. Joe got off of Shelia and began to trash the place. The plan was for him to make it look like a robbery, but Joe had other plans once he looked down at Shelia's perky breasts and shapely figure in the middle of the floor." I gotta fuck this bitch," he said to himself, then made his way over to the body." Damn this shit good," he moaned as he looked down at her. Before it was all said and done, Joe had his way with her in every hole imaginable.

$ $ $

"Damn," Fuzzy cursed when the ringing of her cell phone woke her out of her dream. Her and Speedy were lying out on a beach in Aruba, making love under the moon light. She was just about to bust a nut." Hello," she yelled into the phone. Her anger was quickly replaced with worry when the caller informed her that Big Mama's Kitchen was not open for business yet, since Shelia had told her the day before that she was going in early to prepare for business." It will be opened in the next hour," Fuzzy promised, then ended the call." Come on, Shelia, answer the phone," Fuzzy begged as she got sent to Shelia's answering machine for the third time. Usually Shelia would pick up on the second ring once she realized that it was Fuzzy calling. That's what made Fuzzy call Slim. He could hear the worry in Fuzzy's voice. If there was one thing Slim didn't want, it was for Fuzzy to stress over anything he could prevent.

"Aye, Murph," he called out to one of his men. Murph was a guy that Slim met in the feds at Bennettsville-FCI when he did a small bid for tax evasion. Slim had watched him work out like a work horse day after day. After finding out he was a homie from Rocky Mount, they became cool. When it was time for Slim to leave, they exchanged information and kept in touch, and when Murph got released, Slim put him as head of his muscle team that he sent out when it was time to collect on an overdue debt or when he needed to send a deadly message to someone.

"What's good?" Murph asked when he entered Slim's home office.

"I need you to go by Shelia's and check up on her. Fuzzy said she's not answering her phone and hasn't opened the restaurant this morning."

"I'm on it," Murph replied, then stepped out of the office to get his right-hand man, Forty, a young and crazy gunner from around the way.

"As soon as I hear something I'ma give you a call," Slim informed his niece as he watched Murph and Forty on the security monitor sitting on his desk. Fuzzy agreed, even though deep down in her soul she had a bad feeling that something terrible had happened to Shelia.

Several minutes later, Murph parked his LS 450 in front of Shelia's condo then killed the engine."

Come on," he ordered Forty then hopped out of the car and headed to the back. Forty jumped out of the car and followed suit with his gun drawn. Even though it was mid-summer, the two killers were dressed in all black from head to toe. Murph noticed the broken glass on the back door as well as it being partially open. He held up a finger, signaling for Forty to keep quiet and follow close behind him.

"Oh shit," Murph cursed when he made it to Shelia's bedroom and saw her sprawled out in the middle of the floor naked.

"You want me to call the ambulance?" Forty asked, pulling out his cell phone. After checking Shelia's pulse, Murph responded.

"Nah, we ain't got time for that." Murph picked Shelia's limp body up in his arms and rushed her out of the condo. When they got to the car, Murph handed Forty the keys and hopped in the backseat with Shelia.

"Yo, boss, it's not good," Forty informed once he got Slim on the line. After he told Slim how they had found her and where they were on their way to, he ended the call.

$ $ $

After Fuzzy ended the call with Slim, she went into the bathroom to take a shower. Feeling a little better when she finished, she began to clean the mansion. That was a habit she had ever since she was a little girl coming up. Whenever she got scared, stressed, or worried, she started to clean up. Even when things were already clean. That's what always gave her away when it came to her father, Mr. Biggs. Fuzzy smiled just thinking about those days. That was until her cell phone went off. "Damn." Fuzzy dropped the handle of the vacuum cleaner then snatched the phone from the clip on her hip. "NOOOOO!" she screamed when Slim told her the bad news.

"I'll have my driver come get you and have the

nanny sent over to watch the kids," Slim informed. Thirty minutes later, there was a knock at Fuzzy's door. After viewing the security monitor, Fuzzy hit the entrance button and allowed the nanny, Maria, to enter.

$ $ $

The first face Fuzzy saw when she entered the lobby of the emergency room was Slim's." Everything is going to be okay, princess," Slim promised as she ran into his awaiting arms and he held her tight. Slim's words did little comforting because Fuzzy knew that after being raped, drugged, and beaten, nothing was ever going to be alright or the same from that moment forth. Wilson was just like every other small city. Within the hour of Shelia being rushed into surgery, half the city was there to give their condolences, assumptions of what may have happened, or to be downright nosey. The entire lobby was crowded and noisy. That was until Slim raised his hand up and demanded silence." I got fifty thousand on the head of whoever did this to Shelia," he promised. He wanted to set an example on whoever violated their family/crew. Fuzzy watched as everyone made their exit to put their ears to the street to try to come up with as much helpful information as possible to assist in the bounty.

"I want to see her," Fuzzy told her uncle.

"You will, princess," he promised her, then led her away from everyone." There's someone I want you to meet first." Fuzzy followed Slim out of the lobby of the emergency room to his awaiting Bentley Mulsanne.

S awanda felt like a suspect in the interrogation at the Wilson County Police Department as she sat in the dining area of Big Mama's Kitchen as Slim and Fuzzy drilled her with question after question about the night before when she told them she dropped Shelia off at home. "Yes, I'm positive that no one followed us," she assured them.

"How do you know?" Fuzzy asked doubtfully.

"Because Shelia made me circle the block twice before I parked in front of her condo," she replied honestly. Fuzzy knew Sawanda was telling the truth about that because Speedy used to do the same thing before pulling up in the mansion's driveway. That was something he always stressed to every member of their crew so they would never get caught slipping.

Slim was about to ask Sawanda an important question, when his cell phone rang.

"Umm, huh, at six tonight, we'll be there," was all Slim said before he ended the call." This meeting is over." He directed his attention back to Sawanda, dismissing her. She stood to her feet and made her way to the front exit of the restaurant. That's when she heard Slim say," Fuzzy, go in the back office to the safe and grab a half a million out so we can make this drop at the warehouse beside the old Nichol's Building," making sure Sawanda heard him before she made it out the door. Once Fuzzy was sure Sawanda had pulled out of the parking lot, she reappeared.

"So you think she's going to go for it?" she asked Slim with an evil grin on her face.

"Let's hope for her sake that she don't," he answered as Hadji emerged from the back of the building, surprising Fuzzy.

Before Slim got a chance to ask her a question, Hadji asked one of his own:" But what if she didn't have anything to do with what happened to Shelia but falls for the old banana in the tailpipe trick anyway?" Slim sat and pondered over the question then smiled.

"That means she is a snake anyway for trying to bite the hand that feeds her and she deserves what's going to come to her," he answered, then pulled out a Cuban cigar.

"So that's who Slim was talking to on the phone," Fuzzy thought as she listened to Slim and Hadji conversate. She had to admit that it was a clever plan. Her thoughts were interrupted by the ringing of her cell phone." Excuse me please," she said politely, then made her way to the other side of the restaurant. Hadji watched Fuzzy's ass shake all the way until it was out of view. It was times like that that Hadji doubted the decision he made to settle down. He was brought back to the present by the sound of Slim's voice.

"Have you made your decision yet?" Slim had been trying to get Hadji to join their family over the years but he had always declined, even after he offered to let him take over his position as the head because he knew that's what his brother, Mr. Biggs, would have wanted. Also he wanted Hadji's help on finding out who the new player in the game was, who went by the name of B.B. After revealing his reasons of not joining the family, Slim laid off of Hadji for a while, but now he needed him more than ever.

"No," Hadji said firmly." I haven't come up with my final decision yet." He smiled, knowing Slim thought he had declined him once again. Slim returned the smile and inhaled his cigar." But I will find out who did that to Shelia, not only for you, but also because I owe it to Speedy and Menace. She was like an aunt to all." Hadji looked into Slim's eyes and he could see the hurt that Slim felt in them. Being that Hadji was a little older than the rest of the crew, he remembered the days when Shelia was in her prime, when Slim use to display her on his arm.

"Thank you, nephew," Slim replied gracefully. Little did they know, Fuzzy ended her call a while ago and was ear hustling their entire conversation. Even though she was very small back then, she could see the sparkle in Shelia's and Slim's eyes whenever they were in the presence of each other.

"I should have an address for you in the next hour," Hadji assured Slim as Fuzzy cleared her throat and made her presence known. After Slim nodded his acknowledgment, Hadji turned and headed to the back exit.

"As soon as I hear something, I'ma give you a

call," Slim told Fuzzy then kissed her on both cheeks. She watched as Slim walked out the door, flanked by Murph and Forty. Then she rushed to the back exit to try to stop Hadji.

"Hadji," she called out from the back door as he lifted his car door. Hadji turned around to find Fuzzy speed walking in his direction. He had to look straight ahead to get his eyes off of her camel toe as she approached.

"What's up?" he managed to say after forcing himself to look at her face. He couldn't believe the effect Fuzzy was having on him. He hadn't felt an attraction like he was feeling for another woman since the first day he meet his wife Sherry.

"I just wanted to give you my number." Hadji was about to decline but Fuzzy cut him off. "Just in case you can't get in touch with my uncle with the address or your decision," Fuzzy lied. She secretly prayed that he would call her, for anything. She went into her handbag and pulled out a card with her cell number on it. When Hadji flipped it over, it also contained the number to the mansion Hadji placed the number in his pocket then hit the automatic start on his key fob.

"Will do," Hadji replied then slid down into the driver's seat. When Hadji pulled the door down to close it, he happened to look over in Fuzzy's direction. He found himself shaking his head in disbelief at how shapely she was. "Damn," he cursed just as Fuzzy turned around before she opened the back door to the restaurant. They locked eyes for a few seconds until Fuzzy put on her beautiful smile and slid into the building. Hadji went into his pocket and pulled out the card Fuzzy had given him. He knew that calling her would be like playing with fire. He just wondered if he'd be able to stop the burn.

$ $ $

As soon as Sawanda pulled out of Big Mama's parking lot, she picked up her cell phone and called B.B. "I got some good information that I'm sure will be profitable to both of us," she claimed.

"I'm listening," B.B. replied then put the cell on speaker as Stacy entered the bedroom soaking wet. B.B. was totally distracted by Stacy's flawless body swaying across the room. She stopped at the foot of the bed, lifted her right foot on top of it, then ran her fingers down the middle of her neatly shaved vagina.

B.B. had forgotten all about Sawanda on the phone until she mentioned a half of a million dollars." Say what?" B.B. asked in disbelief," When?" After running down what she had overheard Slim say, B.B. promised to give her a call back in thirty minutes. B.B. sat in the middle of the bed in deep thought." Who can I trust to do a job this big?" B.B. said out loud, catching Stacy's attention.

"How about my brother Ant? You know he keep trying to get down with you and the Jersey Boyz." B.B. thought about it for a while before giving Stacy the green light to call him. Once Stacy got Ant on the phone, B.B. ran down the plan to him, leaving out the amount.

"If you get this right, consider yourself on the team," B.B. promised him. Lucky for Ant, he was Stacy's older brother, because under any other circumstances, B.B. would leave him slumped after he turned over the briefcase. That was like music to Ant's ears. He was going to take full advantage of the opportunity in front of him. Unlike Hadji, who never gave Ant the chance to prove his loyalty, Ant was going to show B.B. just what a real soldier could do. As soon as Ant ended the call, he called up two of his flunkies to put the plan in motion

$ $ $

Ant pulled the stolen Nissan Sentra around the corner from the old abandoned Nichols warehouse at ten minutes til six and saw a Lincoln Continental occupied by two people just like B.B. promised. All y'all got to do is run up on the car, pop the people inside, and recover the briefcase," Ant ordered Mikey and Lil Tee.

Mikey and Lil Tee were two young and hungry stick-up kids from Ant's neighborhood. Being that the two were easily influenced, Ant promised them two thousand dollars apiece for the lick.

"We got you, big homie," Mikey claimed as he pulled the ski mask over his face. Lil Tee did the same, and after checking their clips they hopped out of the Sentra and headed around the corner to put in the work.

"There they are right there," Lil Tee pointed out. Mikey watched the idling Lincoln for a few seconds before making his move.

"Let's go," he ordered his homie, then jetted

toward the car.

"This is going to be the sweetest lick of them all," Lil Tee swore right before he grabbed the door handle on the driver's side. KA-BOOM! The loud explosion could be heard from blocks away. That's what alerted Ant to the fact that something wasn't right.

"What the fuck?" he said to himself as he drove past the burning Lincoln along with body parts from his two flunkies. "Damn, damn, damn," he cursed, slamming his fist against the steering wheel each time. Not because he had lost the valuable players on his team, but because he knew the chance of him joining B.B.'s team now was slim to none.

$ $ $

After Hadji debated on whose number to call after he got the address where Sawanda went once she left Big Mama's Kitchen, he decided on the safest call. "Nice work." Slim nodded then ended the call to call Fuzzy.

A smile came across Fuzzy's face when Slim called her and gave her the address where Sawanda was. She had a feeling deep down in her heart that something wasn't right about Sawanda, she just couldn't put a finger on it. Fuzzy got dressed in black army fatigues, black gloves, and a pair of black Timbs. It had been a while since Fuzzy put in some work, not since she killed K-ROCK for killing her husband Speedy, and she was dying to try out the new Derringer Slim had bought for her when she returned from Atlanta. Fuzzy went into the garage and hopped in the black Rubicon, the one Speedy drove when it was time to do his dirt.

$ $ $

Sawanda was in her living room on her laptop looking at a Good2Go handbag and purse set when the sound of the doorbell caught her attention. "Who in the hell is that?" she wondered as she got up from her spot on the couch. "I'm coming," she yelled out to the person on the other side of the door as it rang again. She hoped it wasn't her ex. If it was she was going to curse his ass out for stalking her. Sawanda swung the door open, ready to let whoever was on the other side have it, until she saw Fuzzy dressed like she was ready to go to Saudi Arabia.

"Aren't you going to invite me in?"

"My fault girl," Sawanda apologized. "I thought you were my crazy ex stalking a bitch and shit."

Sawanda turned around and led the way down the hall. Sawanda went on and on about nothing until she reached the doorway of the living room. That's when she turned around and saw Fuzzy with a gun pointed to the middle of her forehead. Before she got a chance to scream, Fuzzy delivered a single shot that silenced Sawanda forever.

Fuzzy looked over at the laptop's screen and noticed what Sawanda was looking at. "You won't be buying no Good2Go bags today," she laughed. Once she made it to the front door, she took out a rag and wiped the knob down then made her exit. Fuzzy stepped out of Sawanda's apartment then headed down the walkway. She looked around to see if there were any prying eyes on her. Satisfied that there wasn't, she made her way two buildings down to the black-on-black Rubicon. Once Fuzzy started the truck, she reached into her pocket and pulled out her cell phone. "It's done," she notified Slim then ended the call. As she pulled away from the curb, she took one last look over at the apartment as she passed, a wicked smile creased her lips thinking of the work she had just put in.

On the way home Fuzzy couldn't shake the thought of Hadji out of her head. No matter how much she cleaned, rode around, sang, or played the piano, her mind always reflected back to Hadji and what he might be doing at the time. He even appeared in her dreams when she tried to escape by going to sleep. "Girl get yourself together," she tried to tell herself, followed by saying, "He's a married man, Chantel." She often thought about the many ass-kickings she'd handed out to chicks that thought they could throw themselves at Speedy when they thought she wasn't looking. They all quickly learned how wrong they were when they found themselves getting picked up off the ground. Fuzzy laughed at her thoughts as she pulled the jeep back into the garage. After getting herself together, she jumped in her G55 and headed to the hospital to sit with Shelia. She wanted her to be the first face she saw when she came to.

"My nigga," Lil Man shouted over the loud music at his partner then slid into the VIP booth that him and Tank always occupied. The Elite Section of club Drama was only for the boss of bosses, the rich and famous, and of course their guests. Tank reached over the table and dapped his partner up.

"How you holding up?" Tank asked, looking into Lil Man's eyes. Shelia was more than just someone that use to cook up coke for the crew; she was more like a mother figure to a lot of them, especially Lil Man since he had known her longer than any of them had.

"I'm good," he answered and took the bottle of Belve' out of the bucket of ice then cracked the seal. Tank watched Lil Man turn the bottle straight up in the air before placing it down in front of him. "We gotta find out who did this to her."

"We will," Tank agreed, then picked up the bottle of Cîroc he was drinking and turned it up. It was half empty when he placed it back down on the table. "Have you heard anything on that nigga B.B.?" Lil Man asked, changing the subject.

"Nah, man. It's like that nigga some kind of ghost or something. Nobody don't even got a physical description on him, where he hang out at, not even who the nigga's broad is, nothing," Tank confessed. They both sat in silence for the next five minutes sipping on their bottles, pondering over the situation on their hands until a mysterious woman at the bar caught Tank's eyes. Lil Man's eyes followed his partner's. Impressed, Lil Man encouraged Tank to approach her.

"Go handle your business, playa. We'll finish this up tomorrow." Tank heard every word Lil Man said but said nothing. His thoughts were on how much the woman at the bar reminded him of their sixth-grade school teacher they use to lust over in class all day. After finally acknowledging his partner, Tank dapped him up then made his way over to the bar. "My fault, homie," Lil Man apologized after brushing shoulders with a stranger as he headed toward the elevator. The stranger made quick eye contact then nodded before pulling the black Nets fitted down low and heading in the direction of the restroom. The hairs on the back of Lil Man's neck stood up as he watched the stranger walk off. Lil Man tried to figure out where he knew the stranger from, but couldn't. Just as he was about to follow the stranger to the restroom, the elevator bell sounded indicating the elevator door was about to open.

When Lil Man stepped off the elevator back onto the lower level, he headed straight to the bar area to get another bottle before calling it a night. He knew Meka would be up waiting on him like she did every night, so he wanted to be prepared for the night that lay ahead of him. He had to fight off at least three or four lusty hood rats before he finally made it. "Let me get a bottle of Grey Goose and can of Red Bull," he ordered, then turned his back to the bar to look onto the crowded dancefloor. He thought about how far he and Tank had come over the years. "If only Lucky could be here with us," he said to himself as he heard a familiar voice speak up.

"That'll be eighty-five dollars," Kia yelled out over the loud music. Lil Man turned around to see a happy Kia blushing back at him. He hated to admit it, but she was starting to grow on him. He shook that thought from his head because there was no way in the world that Meka would let either of them live if she ever found out about them creeping around behind her back.

"Put it on my tab," he joked, then cracked the seal and opened the can of Red Bull. As soon as he was about to drink enough to replace it with the Grey Goose, another groupie chick came and sat on the stool beside him.

"Hey, handsome. You trying to buy a young lady a drink?" she flirted, flashing one of the cutest smiles

Lil Man had ever seen.

"Sure," Lil Man replied, looking down at her overly exposed cleavage.

"Let me get a Rum and Coke," the groupie chick ordered, leaning over the bar top in Kia's direction to give Lil Man a clear view of her ass hanging from the bottom of her one size too little miniskirt. Lil Man openly stared at her naked ass with images of hitting her from the back. Kia looked at Lil Man and sucked her teeth before rolling her eyes. She was about to give the groupie a piece of her mind, until Lil Man cut his eyes in her direction.

"Ewwww," Kia frowned, then spun on her heels and walked off to fix the drink.

"What's her problem?" the groupie chick asked Lil Man once she sat back down on the barstool. Ignoring the question, Lil Man asked Smiley her name. "Lovette, but all of my friends call me Love for short," she answered just as Kia returned with her drink. "Thank you." As Love started her conversation back up, Lil Man noticed that Kia was still standing close by staring at her.

"Come on, Love. Let's hit the dancefloor." After quickly downing her drink, Love grabbed Lil Man's hand and led him to the dancefloor. Before they made it all the way, Lil Man bumped into Tank with the school-teacher-looking broad on his arm.

"Yo, me and shorty about to bounce up outta here," Tank told his partner. Lil Man took a look at Tank's company for the night and had to admit that she was finer than he thought.

"Bet. Hit me up in the a.m. when you come out."

"Will do," Tank assured him, followed by a firm handshake and a quick embrace. "Oh shit," he heard Tank say, but when he was about to take a step back and see what his partner was talking about, Tank continued, "Don't look now, but you got company moving in fast from your right." The first person that came to his mind was his girlfriend Meka. When Tank let Lil Man go, he turned around and saw Kia and Love standing face to face in a stare down.

"Damn," he cursed then turned back around, only

to see the back of Tank and his choice for the night walking out of the front of the club. Lil Man stood to the side and watched the stare down turn into an all-out brawl. Instead of breaking it up, Lil Man walked right past them and headed to the back exit where his Cadillac CTS-V awaited him.

$ $ $

After Tank followed his fling for the night to the Super 8 Motel, he checked his clip and made sure it was full then put one in the chamber. Once he hit the start button to kill the engine, he looked over to his left."Damn, I'ma tear that ass up," he thought as he watched her ass bounce with each step she took.

"You gonna sit there and wonder how soft it is, or are you gonna come in and see?" she asked, looking back at it. Tank opened then closed his car door, hit the alarm, and was one step behind her before she even had the chance to throw her overnight bag over her shoulder. "Make yourself at home," she called out behind her as she entered the bathroom to freshen up. Once the door closed behind her, the first thing Tank did was open the closet door to make sure no one was inside. He had heard so many stories about niggas getting caught with their pants down. That was the last way he wanted to go out. After he checked the closet, he made his way over to the bed to look underneath it. He laughed to himself thinking how paranoid he was.

"Cool out," he told himself then sat at the foot of the queen-sized bed and grabbed the remote control off the nightstand. He began channel surfing until he found what he was looking for. "Here we go," he smiled as he took off his Timbs. He watched a small Asian woman get banged out by three mandingo looking men.

Twenty minutes later, his company for the night emerged from the bathroom in her birthday suit holding her overnight bag. Tank openly drooled at the mouth. She walked so lightly over to the bed, it was as if she was floating on air. After sitting the overnight bag on the floor beside the bed, she made her way over to the mini-fridge in the corner of the room and opened it. "You going to have a drink with me?" she asked, bending over to grab a bottle of white wine out of the fridge. Tank was too much in a trance to even respond. "I'll take that as a yes," she giggled when she turned around and found out what had Tank's attention. Once she fixed both of them a glass, she went over and sat beside Tank on the bed.

"So what else do you got in that bag, Ms. Stacy?" Tank asked curiously, finally remembering her name.

"I thought you would never ask!" Stacy answered mischievously. She set her glass of wine on the nightstand then leaned over toward the overnight bag on the floor. Tank eased his hand toward his waistline and rested his hand on his pistol. He silently prayed that she didn't try anything crazy because he wasn't going to hesitate if he had to put a hot one in her head. "You wanna play?" she asked, coming up with a pair of handcuffs in her hand.

"Damn, this bitch a real freak," Tank thought to

himself as he watched Stacy stand between his legs.

"I want play whatever you wanna play."

"Is that right?" Stacy looked into Tank's lust-filled eyes then dropped to her knees. "Ummm," she moaned after tasting Tank's pre-cum. It drove him crazy when she released him from her mouth and made a loud popping sound. This time when she placed it back into her mouth, she went to work. She sucked him so good that he slid to the middle of the bed trying to get away. He'd had some monstrous head in his life, but not quite like hers. Feeling himself about to bust, he pushed her head back.

"Let me hit it from the back," he demanded, then raised up on his knees. Stacy was hesitant at first because she knew it was going to be a task taking all of him in her vagina since she couldn't fit all of him in her mouth.

"Fuck it, I came this far," she said to herself thinking of the bigger picture at the end of the rainbow. She would do any and every thing to please B.B., but this would be by far the most painful. She just prayed Ant would barge in before Tank did too much damage. Stacy took in deep breaths as Tank eased in inch by inch until he filled her hole all the way up. By the time she got her rhythm, Tank kicked it into another gear, one Stacy wasn't quite ready for." Oh my God," she swore as Tank vigorously beat her insides. It felt like she could feel him in her chest." I-I-I'm cumming," she cried out in pleasure and pain.

"So am—" Tank started to say, but the impact from Ant's .40 caliber pistol put a stop to it.

"Damn, nigga, what took you so long?" Stacy whispered in a weak voice pushing Tank's dead weight body from on top of her. She didn't want to admit it, but Tank's sex game was the best she'd ever had.

"Wake yo bitch ass up," Ant barked as he took the butt of his pistol and smacked Tank across his face.

Tank had to wipe the blood from his eyes and try to focus his sight on the first person he saw." You dead, bitch," he promised before turning his attention to the man with the gun in his hand." You might as well go ahead and kill me because I ain't giving you shit, nigga," Tank swore, then spat in Ant's face.

"Bitch-ass nigga," Ant shouted, then began pistol whipping Tank over and over again. If it wasn't for Stacy reminding him of the reason they were there, he would have killed him then." Where that bitch Fuzzy rest her head?" Tank looked through bloodshot eyes and managed to smile.

"Both of y'all just signed y'alls' death certificate." Seeing that they were getting nowhere fast, Ant put a bullet in the chamber and shot Tank in the middle of his forehead.

"What a waste of some bomb-ass dick," Stacy thought to herself as she gathered her belongings. When she finished, she watched Ant pour gas on Tank's body then wipe the place down before throwing acid all over him to clean Stacy's DNA.

Stacy sat on the phone talking to B.B. as she watched Ant hop into the passenger seat." Here." She shoved the phone in Ant's direction then rolled her eyes.

"What's good?" Ant asked as Stacy backed out of the parking space and headed to the exit of the lot. Ant listened to B.B. ask question after question before he ended the call. Even though B.B.'s voice was calm, Ant knew B.B. was upset. He just hoped the money he had to offer that he had taken from Tank would make things better.

"Where you want me to drop you off at?" Stacy asked her brother.

"B.B. wants to see me now," he answered. Stacy silently said a prayer for her brother because she knew if B.B. was requesting for him to come over, he might not make it out alive.

To Stacy's surprise, when her and Ant walked into her house, B.B. was not mad at all, after hearing everything Ant had to say." And here's the money he had on him. It's just under ten grand." B.B. looked at the money and told Ant that it was his for putting in the work." So am I in?" he questioned nervously.

B.B. looked into Ant's eyes before answering."

Yeah, you're in." After dapping Ant up and a quick

embrace, B.B. headed out the door to handle some

important business. B.B. thought about sending Ant,

but decided against it since it was personal.

$ $ $

Once Stacy dropped Ant at his car and pulled off,

he got in his car and started it up. Being that B.B. let

him keep all of the money that he had taken off of

Tank, he decided to go out and splurge with some of

his newfound wealth. He hated the fact that his

flunkies had gotten themselves killed earlier on in the

day because now he had to figure out how he was

going to get his hands on a freak for the night since

they always went out to find some for them. He was

sitting at the light on Lodge and Walnut, when he

looked up ahead of him and saw a sexy tall chick

with thunder thighs walking over the train tracks.

"Damn, dat bitch finer than a muthafucka," he said

out loud. As soon as the light turned green, he applied

pressure to the gas pedal and raced up beside her. "What's up, shorty?" Ant rolled down his window and asked, even though she was far from being short. Shorty swayed her hips from side to side as she made her way over to the passenger side window. Her ass was so big, Ant could see it from the front.

"You," she replied as she leaned down and stuck her head down into the window and placed the ice pop she was sucking on back in her mouth. Ant had the AC so high, she had to squint her eyes so they wouldn't get dried out. Ant watched as shorty suck, licked, and slurped the ice pop, and wished it was him.

"Is that right, Kelly?" he asked after reading the name plate that hung from her necklace.

"Umm-hmmm," she shot back, then licked her sticky lips. Ant took his hand off the steering wheel to adjust his hard-on. "How you know my name?" she questioned after making a loud popping sound when she removed the ice pop from her mouth. Hearing that pop damn near made Ant cum on himself.

"Get in," he demanded, and hit the unlock button on the driver's side door. Ant watched Kelly as she placed her thick thighs into the car and sat her phat ass down on the butter-soft leather seat.

"Dis shit is nice," Kelly admitted as she squirmed in her seat to get comfortable.

"I'ma tear dis pussy up," Ant declared then took his eyes off of her camel toe and pulled off down the street. He made a U-turn, went over the bridge, then made a right on highway 301. He made a stop at the liquor store, and since he was in the same area, he decided to go to Powell Street and grab an ounce of weed along with a few X pills while he was at it. That way he could keep Kelly up in the room all night while he did his thing.

After sexing Kelly into a coma, Ant took a shower, got dressed, then headed to his car. The first thing he was going to do was check up on his baby mama. After that he was going to check up on his trap house. As soon as he started the car, his cell phone rang. "What it do, boss?" he answered when he saw B.B.'s number pop up on the screen.

"You trying to go hit up the strip club?" B.B. owned a strip club in Jersey and since coming back to NC had become a little home sick.

"Hell yeah," Ant replied, not wanting to miss out on a chance with hanging with the big dawg.

"Bet. I'll come by your spot to pick you up in thirty minutes," B.B. told him then ended the call. Ant looked at his watch.

"Man, fuck my baby mama," Ant concluded then put his car in drive. Before he could make it out of the parking lot, he noticed the room light pop on. He was about to turn around, until he thought about all the weed, liquor, and X pills he left for her. "That should hold her ass til I return." With that, Ant jumped on the highway and headed to the spot to party with the boss.

After a memorable night at the strip club, B.B. dropped Ant back at his spot with instructions to stop by the Jersey Boyz trap house by noon and pick up his first package. Ant hopped into his car and watched B.B. pull away. That was the opportunity Ant had been waiting on for years. He started his car and headed back to the room to celebrate on the sexy young thing waiting on him.

"What the fuck?" Ant said to himself as he stood outside of the room door patting his pockets in search of the key card. At first he thought Kelly might have had the television up loud on the Playboy channel, until he put his ear to the door and the familiar, sexy moans from Kelly serenaded through the air clearly. "This bitch must got me fucked up," he swore, then pulled out the P90 Ruger from his waistband and put one in the chamber. All he could think about was all the weed, liquor, and X pills that he had just bought her. "Bitches ain't never satisfied," he mumbled as he slid the key card into the slot. As soon as the red light turned green he eased his way into the room. The further he went, the more upset he became. He could hear all kinds of sucking and slurping in the air. When the two figures on the bed came into view,

Ant lowered his gun and watched. "Damn." Kelly lay on her back spread-eagle in the middle of the bed with another chick between her legs eating her out. He couldn't tell what the other chick looked like, but he didn't care. The way her shiny black ass rotated in the air, she could've looked like a mud duck and he still was going to give her the business. Kelly looked into Ant's lust-filled eyes and summoned him over with her finger then inserted it in her mouth.

"Yeah, right there Trina," Kelly coached when Trina hit her spot. Ant unloosened the drawstring to his jogging pants and made his way across the room. By the time he reached the foot of the bed, his jogging pants were down to his ankles. He guided his erection into her wetness with his left hand while still holding his pistol in his right.

"Shhhhhh," Trina sucked in a mouth full of air when Ant entered her from the back. Feeling herself about to cum, Kelly grabbed the back of Trina's head and thrust her hips upward to meet her face. Trina sucked and threw her ass back at the same time without missing a beat.

"Damn this bitch can multitask like a mutha-fucka," Ant admitted as he sped up the pace. The faster he pumped, the faster Trina licked.

"I'm cummmmming," Kelly screamed as creamy wetness shot from her vagina.

"Now it's time to put in work." Trina smiled then threw her ass back at Ant harder and faster, almost making him lose his footing.

"Oh, this bitch wanna play," Ant said to himself then planted both feet into the carpet. Kelly walked over beside Ant while him and Trina went at it like two animals in the wild. Two minutes later, the unimaginable happened.

"I'm about to cum," Ant yelled in defeat, not able to stop himself. Right when he was about to release his load Kelly pushed him back, got on her knees, and put his erection in her mouth. Ant grabbed the back of her head and pumped her mouth vigorously until she swallowed every single drop of his fluids.

"You know you gonna give me some money so I

can get my hair done, right?" Kelly looked up at Ant and said.

"I got you," Ant replied on wobbly legs. Little did she know, for the performance that they just put on, they had won themselves an all-out shopping spree as soon as they got up in the morning. Ant watched Trina grab an X pill off of the dresser then place it in her pussy. Two minutes later, Kelly was facedown between her legs licking her clean.

"Damn, I wish Mikey and Lil Tee were here to witness this shit," Ant thought as he found the strength to crawl over to the twosome and join in.

"Who in the fuck calling my phone this early in the morning?" Lil Man thought to himself, looking at the clock on the nightstand. "Yo!" he spoke into the phone without looking at the caller ID. "What!" he shouted in disbelief, waking Meka from her sleep. She sat up and watched Lil Man with worry as tears began to flow down his face.

"What's wrong?" she mouthed, but Lil Man paid her no mind. He ended the call a minute later then slammed it against the wall, shattering it into little pieces.

"NOOOOO!" he screamed, then jumped out of bed and started getting dressed.

"Baby, what's wrong? Talk to me." Meka slid out of bed and made her way over to Lil Man. He took his keys out of his pocket and tried to walk around her, but Meka stopped him and placed his face in her hands. "Mantrail." Usually when someone called Lil Man by his government name, he got upset, but for some reason, this time it calmed him.

"He's gone, Meka," he looked into her eyes and whispered.

"Who's gone?" she asked, confused. Lil Man grabbed the remote off of the nightstand then turned on the flat-screen.

"Good morning. This is Tyana Moore reporting for WCLN Channel 11 news. I'm outside of room 112 here at the Super 8 Motel." She paused, turning to the side, then pointed at the room behind her. "Earlier this morning the body of an unidentified man was found with a single shot to the middle of his forehead by room service. Anyone with any information please call the number at the bottom of your screen."

Lil Man's sights were on Tank's Audi R8 parked next to the hotel room. Lil Man had no doubt that it was his best friend and partner when the male's arm fell from the gurney exposing the bracelet Tank was wearing the night before. Meka slid the remote from Lil Man's hand then turned the TV off. It pained her to her heart to say what she said next, but she knew it had to be done.

"Go handle your business. I'll be here when you return." Lil Man looked at her and stared into her eyes, then wondered how he could be so blessed to have a woman like her in his life and still fall short in so many other areas.

"I love you," he promised, then kissed her on her lips.

"I love you more," she replied, then watched him walk out the door. She said a silent prayer that he made it back in one piece before Lil Lucky's cry interrupted her.

$ $ $

After driving to Jiffy Mart (Arab Store) to buy a new phone, Lil Man called Slim to reply to the many text messages he had left for him. "I'm on the way," he reported, then ended the call.

Lil Man was greeted by all as soon as he entered club Drama. Everyone sat around the many screens hanging around the bar looking at the surveillance footage from the night before. "I know that chick," Jamontae spoke up, making his way to the bar.

"You sure?" Slim asked.

"Hell yeah I'm sure. I can't forget that pretty-ass face and bangin' body," Jamontae said, remembering the day he got shot down by the beautiful vixen. The only reason he didn't curse her out was because he was on the North Side of town in enemy territory.

"Well what are we waiting for?" Lil Man shouted then headed for the back exit of the club where two black work vans sat, ready to go handle the situation. Slim watched as the crew filed out the back of the club. Just when he was about to leave out the front, his cell began to ring.

"Talk to me, I'll talk back." Slim listened as Hadji relayed the information that Slim requested on who assaulted Shelia. "Good work, nephew," Slim announced before trying to persuade Hadji to join the family, as he did every time he spoke to him.

"I'll get back with you on that, old school." Hadji laughed then ended the call. Slim shook his head from side to side as he thought about what a hard bargain Hadji was giving him. Before placing his phone back on his hip, he made one more call. "You ready to put in some more work?" he asked the caller. Then he read off the address once the caller confirmed what he already knew they would say.

$ $ $

The two black vans crept through the middle-class North Side section of the city that sat right next to the most dangerous hood in town. They hoped they could handle the situation quietly, because they knew if they didn't they might not make it out alive since the only way in and out was through the hood. "That's the bitch's house right there." Jamontae pointed at the two-story brick house.

"You sure that's it?" Lil Man questioned as they passed by.

"Yep," he assured him.

"How you know?" his right-hand man, Diontae, asked.

"Because I followed her home." Diontae knew that Jamontae stalked the woman before because a few times he was riding shotgun. The van erupted in laughter.

"Ain't that her right there?" Diontae pointed as a black-on-black Dodge Charger pulled into the driveway.

"Hell yeah," Flip answered as he watched her step out from the driver seat and walk to the trunk.

"Daaaaaamnn," the crew howled out when she opened the trunk and grabbed two arms full of groceries.

"I would've stalked that bitch too," one of the crew members in the back of the van admitted.

"Come on, let's go," Diontae ordered. He then slid the door to the van open. The crew members in both vans rushed up to the house and through the front door just as Stacy was about to get the rest of the bags out of the trunk.

"What the fuck are y'all doing in my house?" she shouted, looking at the unmasked men like they had lost their minds. "B.B. will have all of your heads for this shit here." Stacy reached for her cell phone that rested in the clip on her hip, but the smack upside her head from Diontae's four-fifth knocked her dizzy and she fell to her knees.

"Get that bitch up and take her to the living room," Jamontae ordered. Diontae grabbed Stacy by her hair and drug her down the long hallway until he came to the living room.

After forcefully slinging her onto the middle of the floor, Jamontae walked up on her and said, "Call B.B."

Stacy looked Jamontae in his eyes as she debated doing what she was told. She could tell Flip to go to hell and deal with whatever consequence he had in store for her, or she could make the call, option number one. "Fuck you," she shouted then closed her eyes and braced for the punishment.

"Big Al," he called out to the three hundred pound beast that stood off to the side. Big Al walked over to Stacy and swung with all of his might.

$$$

"What happened?" Stacy asked twenty minutes later when she came to. Her head felt like it had just been smashed with a jack hammer.

"This will be my last time telling you," Jamontae warned calmly. Then he looked over in Big Al's direction. Stacy looked over at Big Al rubbing his knuckles into the palm of his hand. She lowered her head in defeat and took her phone out of the clip.

"Hello," B.B answered the call on the second ring.

"Someone wants to talk to you." Stacy handed Flip the phone, who in turn handed it over to Lil Man, who stood quietly to the side and observed.

"Now are you ready to talk to a underling?" Lil

Man smirked, feeling like he had the upper hand on B.B.

"Huh," B.B. huffed. "You young boys will never learn. Let me take you to school. You think you have the upper hand, don't you?" Lil Man listened, wondering where B.B. was going with it. "The love of my life was taken from me a few years ago, so I don't give a fuck what you do to that bitch." Lil Man could hear the coldness in B.B.'s voice. "You will be saving me a lot of time and effort if you just go ahead and kill the bitch for me!" Lil Man took out his gun and placed it to the middle of Stacy's head. "Your wish is my command," he stated. B.B. could hear Stacy in the background pleading for her life before the line went dead. Right when Lil Man was about to pull the trigger, Stacy's last comment caught his attention. "I know who raped the lady Shelia that runs Big Mama's Kitchen," she screamed in the nick of time. Lil Man lowered the gun from her head and looked at Stacy sideways.

"What did you just say?" he questioned to make

sure he heard her right.

Stacy looked up with teary eyes and repeated herself.

"Who?"

"It was B.B.'s brother Joe," she told him. The name didn't ring a bell with Lil Man, but he was going to find out. After Stacy gave him the address to Joe's trap house, as well as to her own brother, Ant, Lil Man took her out of her misery.

"Damn, I didn't even get none of that pussy," Jamontae thought to himself as he looked at Stacy's panties peeping from underneath her hiked-up skirt and then followed Lil Man back out to the black van they came in.

"So where to now?" Diontae asked from the back of the van as they pulled away from Stacy's house and through the rough projects at the beginning of the suburban neighborhood.

"To pay Mr. Joe a little visit." Lil Man lay back in his seat then lit the blunt that rested in his mouth.

$ $ $

After receiving the call from Slim, Fuzzy put on her black fatigues and jumped in the all black Rubicon then headed to the address that he gave her. She knew Hadji had given Slim the address, and for the life of her she couldn't figure out why he hadn't called her. "Maybe he don't want me getting into any trouble," she reasoned, then smiled on the inside. Just thinking about him got her tingly all over. "Snap out of it, girl," she told herself, coming up on the address she put in the navigation system. When she looked up, she noticed a guy walking up the street that fit the description Slim had given her. Thinking quick, Fuzzy hopped out of the jeep and popped the hood.

"You need some help with that, sexy?" Joe asked, noticing her phat ass sticking out as she bent over under the hood. Fuzzy raised up with a smile on her face.

"Yes, handsome," she replied, taking a step back.

"What is it doing?" Joe asked as he bent under the hood to take a closer look.

"Umm, I don't know. It just stopped working," she responded as she pulled out her Taurus with the silencer at the tip of it. Joe was so into trying to impress the beauty dressed in black that it never dawned on him that she was dressed in black with a pair of black gloves until it was too late.

"Shit," he cursed when he felt the cold steel against the back of his head. Before he got the chance to lift up, Fuzzy splattered his brains all over the motor.

"Damn I got to get one of the guys to clean this shit," she said to herself as Joe's body slid to the concrete. Once Fuzzy got back in the car and put it in drive, she ran over Joe for good measure. "That was for Shelia, you bitch-ass nigga." Fuzzy laughed then headed back home.

$ $ $

B.B. was on the way to pay Joe a visit because one of the Jersey Boyz had called and said that Joe's picture had been all over the news for the assault on the owner of Big Mama's Kitchen. After ending the call, B.B. pressed down on the gas pedal, knowing if the police got to Joe first and put the pressure on him, he was going to tell everything. The only reason B.B. dealt with Joe in the first place was because they were family and he wanted to give Joe the benefit of the doubt. Family or not, B.B. had come too far to let Joe ruin everything. "What the fuck?" B.B. thought, looking down Joe's block at all the police cars and bystanders on each side of the street making it impossible for B.B. to get a clear view at what was going on. "Excuse me, ladies," B.B. called out to two hood rats leaving the scene making their way past the car. "What happened down there?" One of the hood rats came to a halt and glanced at the expensive luxury car then back at the girl she was with before responding.

"That nigga Joe just got his shit pushed back," she admitted as she made her way over.

"Word?" B.B. asked shocked. "Did anyone see who did it?" B.B. asked curiously.

"No, all I saw was the back end of a Jeep bending the corner when I was coming outta my apartment." The hood rat continued talking, but B.B. paid her no mind.

"Do you got a name and number?" the hood rat questioned, glancing over her shoulder at her friend that impatiently tapped her feet against the pavement waiting for her to finish telling the driver what had happened. By the look on her friend's face, B.B. knew they had to be more than just friends.

After B.B. slid her the number, the other hood rat went in on her: "Quita, you gon' disrespect me like this?"

"It wasn't nothing like that," she lied, then made her way back over to the sidewalk to join her friend. B.B. pulled off and headed to HWY 264 to get a room, and never noticed the two vans pass by.

"You want war," B.B. said out loud. "Then it's war you get."

$ $ $

"So how are things going?" Chris asked once B.B. finally answered the call. B.B. had been ducking Chris's call since no good news could be reported.

"I need for you to come bring the Boyz some more toys down as soon as possible," B.B. answered, getting down to business. That was the code for Chris to bring some more guns down from Jersey as soon as possible for the crew.

"Say no more. I'll be there ASAP," Chris responded then ended the call. Chris had been in the streets much longer than B.B. and hated to discuss business over the phone, even though they only talked on throw-aways and changed phones weekly.

After placing the phone on the nightstand beside the king-sized bed, B.B. lay back, looked up at the ceiling fan, and thought about Stacy and all of the fun they had together. Even though Stacy was a true rider, what B.B. missed about her the most was her head game. The ringing of the phone brought B.B. back to the present. "Who dis?" B.B. asked, not recognizing the number on the screen.

"Umm, dis Quita," an unfamiliar voice answered in a low tone. B.B. tried to put a face with the name but kept coming up blank. "The girl that you gave your number to earlier today in Joe's hood," Quita said, trying to refresh B.B.'s memory.

"Oh yeah?" B.B. said out loud, remembering the sexy hood rat on Joe's block. "What's good?"

"I'm trying to see you," she boldly answered. B.B. loved her straightforwardness and decided to see what her head game was hitting for.

"You driving?"

"Yep. Where do I need to come?" After giving Quita the room number, B.B. ended the call and headed to the bathroom to freshen up.

"She play her cards right, she might become the next Stacy." B.B. smiled, thinking about Quita's juicy, wet lips and the many tricks they were about to perform.

Meka hurriedly pulled her Range Rover Sport into the driveway. She had just dropped Lil Lucky off at her mother's house so her mom could watch him for the weekend for her. Meka looked at the Lady Cartier on her wrist and smiled. "One hour," she said out loud after checking the time. That was enough time to go inside and set the scene for the night's events. They loved to role play, and tonight Lil Man was supposed to play the milk man that came over to deliver her milk while her husband was off to work. She hit the start button to kill the engine then hoped out of the front seat. As soon as her feet hit the pavement, she took the key fob into her hand and hit the trunk button. In an instant the hatch to the back of the truck came open. Meka was so busy texting Lil Man that she never noticed the hooded man approaching quickly from the rear, until it was too late. She felt a sharp pain in the back of her head, and right before everything went completely black, she was thrown into the back of her truck.

$ $ $

After B.B. followed Lil Man for an hour straight, they pulled into Big Mama's Kitchen. Lil Man was on the phone the entire time trying to get Kia off his line. She had been trying to get him to come to her apartment to see the new furniture she purchased with the money he gave her. "Okay, damn. As soon as I leave Big Mama's I'll be there." Once Kia accomplished her mission, she ended the call with all smiles. Lil Man shook his head as he walked over to the entrance of the restaurant and went inside. He knew that messing with Meka's first cousin was dead wrong, and he planned to put a stop to it as soon as he went over there after the meeting he had with Fuzzy and Hadji. That was, of course, after he got some of her serious head game to take his mind off all the tension he'd been having. If he wasn't thinking with his little head so much, he would've seen the blacked-out SRT-8 Charger following him when he left his house.

$ $ $

"Well I'll be damned," B.B. whispered after laying eyes on Fuzzy. She had just returned from the restroom as Lil Man was taking seat beside the young man she was having dinner with. If it wasn't for the many surveillance cameras everywhere, B.B. would've put an end to their cat-and-mouse game right then and there.

"Be patient," B.B. whispered, thinking of the perfect plan to make them both suffer.

After explaining to Fuzzy and Hadji what went down at Stacy's house right up until B.B. got on the phone, Lil Man told how coldhearted B.B. really was. "I'm telling y'all, the nigga told me to go ahead and kill the bitch, then hung up on me. So I was about to do just that, until she told me B.B.'s brother named Joe did that to Shelia, and her brother named Ant killed Tank!" Before Fuzzy or Hadji got the chance to respond, Lil Man's cell vibrated, indicating that he had an unread text." Excuse me for a sec." He had a feeling that he was definitely about to get an earful.

"What's the matter?" Fuzzy asked once she looked over at Hadji, who had his face all balled up like he was ready to kill someone. Just as Hadji was about to tell her, Lil Man returned.

"I'll holla at y'all later. That was Meka texting me to let me know she's home." He smiled mischievously.

"Go handle your business." Fuzzy laughed, remembering Meka telling her about their roleplay nights they had once a month. Lil Man saluted them both before turning on his heel and heading out of the restaurant. As soon as he was out of sight, Fuzzy brought her attention back to Hadji. "Now. Are you going to tell me why you sitting over there with a look on your face like someone just stole your bike?"

Fuzzy joked to lighten up the mood. Hadji looked over at Fuzzy and put on a fake smile, but she saw right through it. She reached over and placed her hand on his then gave it a slight squeeze." You can talk to me," she encouraged. After exhaling a deep breath, Hadji broke it down to her.

"Do you remember asking me about the guy you and Speedy saw me with at the club that time?" he asked. Fuzzy nodded yes, then he continued." Well that guy had his homie to kill my cousin Sean, the other guy that I was sitting with."

"Wow," Fuzzy whispered in a low tone. Before she got the chance to ask another question he filled her in a little more.

"His homie was the guy Ant that Lil Man said was the actual trigga man that killed Tank." Fuzzy sat stunned. Now things were coming clear to her, but what came out of Hadji's mouth next spoke volumes:" I'm in."

At first Fuzzy thought she had misunderstood him, but once he repeated himself, she knew that she hadn't.

"That's great," Fuzzy admitted with a huge grin on her face." I'll call Uncle Slim later and let him know the good news!" Once they finished their dinner, Hadji stood to leave. "Oh yeah. I'm having a little get together at my place this weekend and you are invited." Hadji looked down into Fuzzy's eyes. He wanted to decline her offer, but when she told him that she would tell everyone about him joining the family then, he accepted.

"Let me see your phone?" Hadji asked with his hand out. Fuzzy pulled out her cell from her handbag then handed it to him. After storing his number, he handed it back to her. She looked at his name and noticed the five stars he placed behind it.

"What do these stars stand for?" she asked.

"That represents general status," he answered." That's the only position I play." He winked, then walked away with authority. Fuzzy watched as Hadji headed to the back where he always made his famous exit. Fuzzy couldn't explain her feelings at the time, but there was one thing she knew for sure, she had to tell someone what she was going through.

$ $ $

Fuzzy left Big Mama's Kitchen to take a ride to clear her mind. Thirty minutes later, she was pulling her Maybach 57 into the entrance of Lane Street Cemetery. After taking a deep breath, she stepped out and walked over to the tombstone. "Mr. Biggs," she read with a smile, thinking of all of the fun times they use to have together. Life seemed so easy and so carefree back then. No worries, no stress, no nothing. Fuzzy picked a single long-stemmed rose from the bouquet she had in her hand and then placed it in front of her father's headstone before letting him know what had been going on in her life as of late." I met your protégé." She blushed just thinking about Hadji. "I'm proud to let you know that he finally joined the family now. I can see why you chose him to follow in your footsteps. He's very humble. He reminds me so much of you," she admitted before changing the subject." Another one of ours took a fall, and it looks like we are about to have to go to war over our turf. Some new guy by the name of B.B. has violated the code in so many ways." She shook her head." Guess what? Shelia gets out of the hospital tomorrow, so she should make it to the cookout we're having so that everyone can meet Hadji." She finished up then told him she would return next month on his birthday. After saying a silent prayer, Fuzzy stood up to her feet, turned on her heels, and then took one step over and was standing in front of Speedy's grave." Hi, Love," she cheered happily. Even though he wasn't there with her in the physical, she could feel him with her mentally." The kids and I miss you dearly. They ask about you constantly too. They are getting sooooo big," she exclaimed, raising her hands up to her chest as if he could see her. Fuzzy talked to him for about an hour before picking off a long-stemmed rose and placing it on his tombstone. She took a deep breath then exhaled because she knew the hardest part of all was coming. Walking over to the next grave plot, Fuzzy kneeled down on one knee and set the rest of the roses in front of it." These are for you, beautiful," she whispered to her best friend, then kissed her hand and touched the front of the headstone. She wished badly that Red could have been there to watch Lil Menace grow up. Jr. and Lil Menace were spitting images of their fathers, and everyone reminded her of it daily." You ain't going to believe this, bitch," Fuzzy claimed, then leaned close to the headstone as if making sure no one else could hear her but Red." I met this fine-ass brother named Hadji." She paused for a second like Red was about to respond, then went on." He was Daddy's protégé before he got killed. The strange thing about him is that he reminds me so much of Daddy." After telling her everything, from the fact that he had joined the family, all the way up to her playing with herself at nights and feeling guilty, as if she was cheating on Speedy, she said her good-byes. "I love you, sis!" she said, and then made her way back to her car to go get the kids from

Slim's.

$ $ $

Before Lil Man went to the house for roleplay night with Meka, he stopped by Kia's like he promised. He knew if he didn't she would be blowing his phone up and possibly stopping by to pretend like she was looking for Meka. She liked to play dangerous like that, and to tell you the truth, Lil Man liked that about her. As soon as he parked his car in front of Kia's place, he got out and headed to the door. Before he even got the chance to find the right key to open the door, Kia swung it open in her birthday suit." Took you long enough." Kia rolled her eyes and turned around, giving Lil Man a full view of her backside." Ouch," she jumped from the sting that came from the slap on her ass that Lil Man delivered to her. When she turned to face him Lil Man pushed her back against the wall and shoved his tongue in her mouth."Mmmmm," she moaned in delight, then wrapped both legs around his waist, and her arms around his neck. Lil Man carried her to the living room and laid her in the middle of the floor, where he commenced to laying his pipe game down on her. She was shocked, since the only thing he let her do was suck him off in the past.

"Put it in my mouth," she begged, then tilted her head back. Lil Man pulled out of her and released every last bit of his juices into her mouth and down her throat. The little bit that didn't make it landed on her breasts, where she rubbed it all in like some lotion. Lil Man lay in the middle of the floor, drained, as Kia got up and walked out of the room to get him something to drink and a rag to wipe himself like she did every time he stopped by to view something new that he had bought for her house." You ready for round two?" she asked when she came back into the room with a glass of Henny in one hand and a warm rag in the other. After downing the glass of Henny straight with no chaser, Lil Man took the rag out of Kia's hand and wiped himself off." What are you doing?" Kia asked when she noticed Lil Man sliding his pants back on his waist.

"Come on, Kia. You know what this is. I got to go home to Meka and my son," he answered, buckling up his pants. Kia looked at Lil Man like he had lost his mind as he fastened his belt.

"This nigga got me fucked all the way up if he think he gonna keep treating me any kind of way," Kia thought to herself as she tried to build herself up to give him the ultimatum that she had been wanting to give him so long. She just hoped that her little plan didn't go south and backfire on her." Look, Lil Man, I'm not feeling this thing we got going on," she began, looking him in his eyes." I'm so much better for you than she is. Why don't you just tell her about us and be done with it?" Kia stared into Lil Man's eyes, hoping he was listening to the words she had just said to him. Kia really did, deep in her heart, love Lil Man, and she hoped he felt the same about her, but the words that came out of his mouth let her know different.

"Kia, there is NO US," he responded calmly."

Like I told you before, I will never leave my family for you or no one else," he repeated to her for the umpteenth time. Lil Man was growing quite tired of playing games with Kia, and he eventually knew that if he kept on, he would lose his family. That was something he wasn't planning on doing. Kia followed Lil Man as he walked out of the living room and down the hall to her front door, all the way until he took her key off of his key ring and placed it on the table beside it. It felt like a knife had just been plunged into Kia's chest.

"So you just gonna leave me alone like dat?" she questioned as tears streamed down her face. Lil Man didn't respond. Instead he opened the door and walked outside. When he got to his car he took one last look before disarming his alarm." Okay, nigga. We'll see what Meka say when I call her and tell her we been fucking," Kia threatened. Lil Man let Kia's threat bounce off his shoulders, and opened the car door." Fuck you, Lil Man." Kia stepped her naked ass back from the doorway then slammed the door shut. After starting the car, Lil Man put it in drive and headed home to make things right with his woman. He just hoped Kia's threat was as empty as they always were. If not, he knew that the one last stop he had to make before he got home would seal the deal

$ $ $

It was unusually quiet when Lil Man entered the home he and Meka shared together for the last two years. It was so quiet, an eerie feeling came over him. After calling her name out twice, he headed up the stairs to their bedroom." What in the fuck?" Clothes, shoes, and various items were sprawled out all over the floor. That was very unusual because Meka was a shoe freak and would never have them out of place. The mattress was even off to the side of the bed as if someone had thrown it off to look under it." Maybe Kia did call Meka and told her all about us," Lil Man thought, He reached for his cell that rested in the clip on his hip." Stupid bitch," he cursed, ready to let her have it. Before he could press the connect button to her name, his phone rang. His heart dropped to the pit of his stomach when a picture of Meka popped up on the screen with the name Wifey under it.

"Lil Man, help," he heard her cry out before the phone was snatched from her ear.

"Mekaaa!" he yelled into the receiver in a panic. After getting no response, he rushed out of the room and down the hallway to the front door.

"Now that I've got your attention. How much does this pretty young thing mean to you?" B.B. asked, rubbing the side of Meka's face.

"If you lay one hand on her I will kill you, nigga," Lil Man threatened. His grip was so tight on the phone, he could hear it cracking in his hand. Lil Man opened the door to get in his car to search for B.B., but he didn't have to go far. Lil Man stared at the tinted-out black-on-black Dodge Charger parked across the street from his house.

"I wouldn't do that if I were you," B.B. warned when Lil Man reached for the gun poking out of his waistband.

"What do you want?" Lil Man asked, slowly removing his hand from the handle of his pistol." Is it money? I'll pay you whatever!" Lil Man listened to B.B. laugh hysterically for a few seconds before answering.

"Nigga, I don't want your short-ass change, because that's all your money is to me, change," B.B. bragged." I want your life for your bitch's life." Lil Man swallowed long and hard. Even though he would give his life for her or their son, he just never imagined that it would come to that.

"Okay, I'll do it," he conceded in defeat.

"I'll call you in forty-eight hours to give you the location," B.B. finalized, then put the car in drive." You have one day to get your affairs in order and play with your son. Oh yeah, and come alone. If I see the police or anyone from your little pissy-ass crew, your bitch is dead," B.B. promised, then stepped on the gas.

"Hello, hello!" Lil Man screamed into the phone as he watched the black SRT8 Dodge Charger jet off down the street. He thought about jumping into his ship to take chase, but he didn't want to take the chance of B.B. killing Meka because of his dumb decision. The thought of calling Fuzzy or Slim crossed his mind but got quickly erased as well." Fuck," he yelled, then turned around and rushed into the house and closed the door. He knew he had to do some serious planning if he planned on getting Meka back. He looked at the wedding ring he pulled from his pocket then kissed it." I promise I'll get you back," he vowed.

$ $ $

After leaving Lil Man standing in his front yard, B.B. drove to Ant's spot to pick him up and give him instructions on what needed to be done at that point. "You think you can handle this, playboy?"

"No doubt," Ant answered. He knew that if he could complete the task without a glitch, he would be in B.B.'s graces. B.B. bent a few corners while giving off command after command before pulling back up in the driveway of the spot. Instead of stopping in front of the spot, B.B. pulled all the way to the back, in front of the bar that sat behind the trap.

"Look in the trunk," B.B. ordered, then killed the engine. Ant got out of the car and headed to the rear of it.

"Oh shit!" Ant spoke with wide eyes as he stared down into the trunk at Meka. She was blindfolded and gagged but still looked stunning. Ant reached down to get her out of the trunk. As B.B. walked to the back of the car, he removed the restraints.

"When Lil Man and the rest of the crew catch up with y'all, y'all gonna be some dead bitches!" Meka promised, then coughed up a mouth full of phlegm and spat it in Ant's face.

"You little—," Ant began, drawing his hand back to slap Meka in her face.

"No!" B.B. stopped him and walked to the back door.

Ant bit down on his bottom lip in an attempt to try to control the beast that lingered within him.

"Come on, bitch." He grabbed Meka roughly by her arm then shoved her in the direction of the house.

"I warned you that she was a feisty one, didn't I?" B.B. laughed once Ant entered the small room. Before Ant closed the door behind him, he gave Meka a hard push in her back that sent her tumbling to the floor.

"Ouch," she screamed, then sat on her butt and held her left skinned up knee. Ant's eyes rested on Meka's pink Victoria's Secret panties." Fuckin' pervert," she shouted, then closed her legs when she realized that her skirt was hiked up showing off her goods. Meka looked at Ant's crotch area and saw his erection growing. "Nooo," she pleaded when she saw the lustful look in his eyes as he slowly walked toward her.

"Take the bitch in the back room," B.B. ordered. A smile came across Ant's face just thinking about the many positions he was going to sex her in. Once B.B. left the room, Ant hoisted Meka up off of the floor and threw her over his shoulders. Meka fought with all of her might when she felt Ant's hands go up her skirt as if he was trying to balance her.

Once Ant laid Meka on the bed, B.B. turned around and headed for the door." I'll give you a call in forty-eight hours with the location for you to bring the girl to." Ant couldn't believe his ears. He was going to have 48 hours to do as he pleased with the beautiful young thang in the middle of his bed. He couldn't stop his dick from jumping in his pants." Trina and Kelly gonna have to wait," he thought to himself. B.B. watched Ant make his way over to the bed with his hardness gripped in his hand like a pistol.

"Ant, don't touch the merchandise," B.B. warned, then left the room.

"Oh well," Ant said to himself. He knew not to disobey B.B.'s orders, so he sat across from Meka on the couch, pulled out his erection, and began to ejaculate. Meka thought she was going to throw up all over herself when Ant started to convulse out of control.

Fuzzy walked out of her bedroom onto the balcony and stared out into her crowded backyard at all of the crew members that came to the cookout. Everyone seemed to be enjoying themselves. The guys were either playing basketball on the full court that Speedy had built for his team to practice on, shooting dice on the outside wall of the barn, or playing cards on the picnic tables that were set up near the grill area, while their wives, girlfriends, or mistresses stood by their sides or in the pool area getting their eat or drink on. It was times like this that made Fuzzy miss Speedy the most. She was brought out of her zone by the sound of the buzzer, indicating that someone was at the front gate awaiting entrance. Even though the black Cadillac

CTS-V was limo tinted out, she knew exactly who was inside. After the gates were far enough apart, Lil Man drove his luxury car onto the premises. She couldn't wait to lay her eyes on Lil Lucky. Every time that she did, instant memories of Lucky rushed back to her. Fuzzy watched Sade rush to the back door of the car and waited for Lil Man to open it so she could take Lil Lucky over to the guesthouse with the rest of the kids at the cookout. She looked like she was just as happy as Fuzzy was, jumping up and down in one spot clapping her hands." I wonder where Meka's at?" Fuzzy thought to herself after Lil Man placed his son on the ground and watched Sade drag him to the guesthouse. Once they were out of sight, Lil Man looked up toward the house.

"Shiiit. Ain't no way I'm walking around this big muthafucka," he claimed, heading to the front door to cut through the house to get to the back.

Fuzzy was just about to go downstairs to greet him, when a bright-yellow vehicle pulled up to the gate. A gigantic smile creased her lips when she saw the driver's jeweled-up wrist reach from the driver's window and hit the buzzer to be buzzed in. Fuzzy quickly ran over to her dresser and made sure her makeup and clothing were in tact before she went back over to the window to watch the man of the day step out of his sports car." Damn, he is fiiinnnneee," she squealed looking from his white and yellow button-up Polo top, to his neatly pressed white Polo shorts with the yellow logo on the back pocket. The matching yellow and white Polo sneakers set his outfit off to the T. She watched him make his way over to the passenger side and lift the door into the air. At first she thought he came to his own celebration bearing gifts, until Sherry (his wife) stepped out looking like a million bucks. Many emotions came over Fuzzy, like envy, hate, hurt, and most of all, jealousy. Even though she knew Hadji had a wife, the thought of him coming to the cookout alone and spending some time talking over drinks crossed her mind a few times, maybe even trying to steal a kiss, but now all of that was ruined. Fuzzy rolled her eyes, stomped her feet, and headed to her walk-in closet. " Ain't no way I'm going to let her outshine me at my place," Fuzzy swore. She knew it was going to be a task since Sherry was sporting an all-white Balenciaga sundress with yellow flower designs all over it. Fuzzy bypassed the same exact dress in her closet that she bought a week prior. The only difference was the one she had, the flowers were decorated in red." Bingo," she smiled when she stumbled upon the perfect dress that complimented her curvy figure.

After changing into a cream-colored Christian Dior summer dress, she spun around in the full-length mirror that hung on her wall. Proud of her selection for the day, Fuzzy exited her room and headed down the stairs.

"There goes my princess," Slim announced when Fuzzy emerged out of the back door of the mansion. The Brazilian twins, Shelia, Hadji, and Sherry all watched her as she approached them. Sherry was actually impressed since the last time she saw Fuzzy at the beauty salon she had just taken her braids out.

"I am so glad you could make it," she addressed Hadji, then diverted her attention to Sherry." And you brought your wifey I see. Nice to see you again, Sherry, if I'm not mistaken, isn't it?" Fuzzy extended her hand out to Sherry for a handshake.

"Yes it is," Sherry answered, accepting Fuzzy's awaiting hand." Fuzzy, right, if I'm not mistaken," she countered. Before Fuzzy could respond, Sherry complimented her on her dress." That is such a beautiful dress."

"I know it is," Fuzzy thought to herself.

"Hadji ordered me the same dress from Italy for my birthday last week," Sherry boasted. Fuzzy could hear the light shade that Sherry was trying to throw her way, and it took everything in her power to stay calm." That was for eyeing my husband when we pulled up," Sherry said to herself when she noticed Fuzzy's handshake tighten." Mission accomplished." Little did Sherry know, Fuzzy was the queen at playing dirty.

"Please call me Chantel, if you will," Fuzzy corrected Sherry before releasing her hand and turning to speak to the twins, who stood by Slim's side. After speaking to Shelia, they shared a short hug and a kiss on each cheek. An awkward moment of silence came over everyone until Slim cleared his throat to get their attention.

"Come, come, everyone." He clapped his hands twice then told them to follow him onto the stage set up for the DJ and his equipment. Once Slim grabbed the mic and said a few words to the DJ, he turned the music completely off so Slim could be heard." Let me get everybody's attention." He patiently waited for all of the crew members to stop what they were doing to gather around to hear what he had to say." I'm glad all of you came to celebrate here with us on this joyous occasion today," he began, and the crew started hooting and cheering. Slim waited for them all to calm down before he continued." I'm sure most of you that have read The Enemy Within already know who this man right here is." Slim waved Hadji over to his side and looked at his brother's (Mr.

Biggs) protégé in admiration." No, he is not a myth,

I assure you. He is alive and kicking as you all are

witnessing." Whispers could be heard throughout the

backyard until Slim held his hand up high, silencing

them all." For those of you that have never heard of

Hadji and his old crew, I assure you, he is not to be

reckoned with and is officially a part of this family,"

Slim let it be known. Hadji looked out at all of the

crew members in attendance. He knew quite a few of

them since he had served most of their brothers'

weight at one time or another. After raising his right

hand in the air and saluting his fellow comrades, he

took a step back. The majority of the crew saluted

back, while the others looked from one to the other

with confused expressions on their faces. Hadji knew

that not everyone was going to take kindly to him just

entering the family and moving up the ladder so

quickly, but it was what it was.

"So what is his rank?" a crew member by the

name of T-Luv asked. T-Luv was a loudmouth,

arrogant member of the crew that always had something to say about everything and everybody. His bark was a hell of a lot louder than his actual bite. He brought plenty of money in, but just as much drama as well.

"Let me answer him," Hadji asked, taking the microphone out of Slim's hand before he had the chance to respond. Slim took a step back and faded out of sight so Hadji could have the stage to himself." My man, what's your name?" he questioned.

T-Luv poked his chest out and spoke up proudly." T-Luv!" he shouted, then took a step closer to the stage. Hadji looked down deep into the young soldier's eyes and immediately knew he would be a major problem in the long run.

"Well, Mr. T-Luv. I'm the new general, and I'm here to let you know personally that your services are no longer needed," Hadji said in his best Nino Brown impression. You could hear many of the crew members whispering under their breaths while the rest of them straight out laughed at the embarrassed look T-Luv had on his face. To save face T-Luv swallowed his pride, put on the meanest mean mug he could muster, and pushed his way through the crowd.

"Bitch-ass nigga," he said a little too loudly, and Hadji heard him.

"I got five Gs on the first person to knock that nigga's block off," Hadji promised to any crew member willing to step up to the plate. T-Luv's heart dropped to his stomach when he looked into the hungry eyes of his so-called homies. It wasn't the money that made them go against their homie, because they threw away a lot more than that on any given night at club Drama. It was the love, loyalty, and respect they had for Slim, Fuzzy, and now their new general, Hadji. Sherry looked on in disbelief as she watched her husband control the crowd. It was the side she had heard about but never had the opportunity to witness firsthand until now. It kind of turned her on, as well as Fuzzy, who loved a man that knew how and when to take control of situations.

154

SMACK, a loud smack resonated through the air, and then a small circle followed. When Hadji looked to see what had happened, he saw T-Luv lying face down as Jamontae and Diontae stomped him out. When they were finished, Lil Man bent down, ran his pocket, then took the Gucci link chain around T-Luv's neck. Hadji smiled as Lil Man walked up onto the stage to get his earnings. Being that Hadji was a man of his word, he reached into his pocket, counted off 50 one hundred dollar bills then extended them to Lil Man.

"Your money ain't no good with me, homie." Lil Man waved his gesture off." We family." Hadji shook his head up and down in admiration then dapped Lil Man up. After their short embrace, Lil Man took a step back and raised the bottle of XO he held in his hand." To family," he announced, then turned the bottle up to his mouth.

"To family," the crew all yelled in unison.

Before everyone went back to the party, Hadji had one more announcement to make." Come on, baby." He held his hand out for Sherry to take it. Once she did he pulled her by his side and wrapped his arm around her shoulder." This is my wife, Sherry, and I would like for y'all to show her the same respect that y'all show Slim, Fuzzy, and me." Hadji looked out into the crowd and watched the expression on everyone's face to see if he could sense any sign of betrayal. He didn't. Once he was satisfied that everyone was on the same page, he handed the microphone back to the DJ and everyone went back to doing whatever it was they were doing before Slim stopped the party.

"Where's Meka?" Fuzzy asked Lil Man after pulling him to the side.

"She wasn't feeling too well, so she had to sit this one out," he lied, hoping Fuzzy just bought his story.

"Oh. Okay. Make sure you tell her to call me when you get home." After agreeing, Lil Man made his way back over beside the barn where the rest of the crew had gone to finish their game of dice. Even though Fuzzy didn't question him any further about

Meka's whereabouts, she made a mental note to give her a call later to see what was up with her because it wasn't like her to not come to a big event.

"There you are," a familiar voice called out, making Fuzzy take her attention from Lil Man. When she turned around, all she could do was smile when she saw who was standing before her with a handful of roses.

"Gary," she cheered. She hugged his neck as tight as she could. Gary was one of Mr. Biggs's closest friends and his hitman before his wife got killed. After that, Gary picked up the bottle of sin and had never been the same. That was until he saw Russo kill Biggs in cold blood and told Slim. Once Slim paid Gary, with the promise for him to leave town and get himself together, Gary did just that.

"Look at you. You're looking good," Fuzzy said after she took a step back and looked Gary up and down. She was telling the truth because Gary used to be one of the best-dressed men she had ever seen, besides her father." How long are you in town for?"

Gary looked at his Rolex for the time then responded," I was just passing through. I will be heading back home when I leave from here," he answered." I brought you these though." Gary handed Fuzzy the twelve long-stemmed roses. She could tell Gary was feeling a little uncomfortable being around so many strangers, even if they were family.

"Come on. Let me walk you out." Fuzzy intertwined her arm with his and led the way to the back door to take the shortcut to the front.

"Isn't that—"

"It can't be—," was heard as they walked through the crowd. Many of the crew members had heard of the hood legend, but thought he had gotten killed years ago or had drunk himself to death. When they reached the back door, Gary turned around and spotted Slim and Hadji off in the distance. After saluting them both, Gary turned and walked into the mansion with Fuzzy leading the way.

Thirty minutes after Slim and the Brazilian twins

left the cookout, Hadji decided to call it a day as well." Where's your bathroom?" he asked Fuzzy once he finally found her. After giving him the long directions that she knew would make him take forever to find it, she went back to doing whatever she was doing. She watched as Hadji bent down and whispered a few words in Sherry's ear before he headed into the mansion. Once she was sure no one was watching her, she made her way to the other side of the mansion and entered through the side door.

Once Hadji finished relieving himself, he washed his hands and looked around. He had to admit that Fuzzy's mansion was the shit. Even though his mansion was a nice size, Fuzzy's was huge. Where small things such as the shower head, faucet handles, and door knobs at Hadji's mansion were silver or even gold, Fuzzy's were all platinum. Hadji was damn near afraid to touch the doorknob to get out of the bathroom, but when he did, he came face-to-face with Fuzzy.

"I thought you might have gotten lost," she said

with a big smile on her face.

After putting on his million-dollar smile, Hadji creased his lips to respond. " Nah, I was just—" he began, but was silenced when Fuzzy's soft lips pressed against his. Before he could close his mouth, Fuzzy forced her tongue down his throat, pushed him back inside the bathroom, and shut the door behind them with her foot." Fuzzy—" he tried to speak, but the rest of his sentence was cut short when she reached down into his shorts and grabbed his throbbing erection. Hadji began kissing her back until they were interrupted by a knock at the door.

KNOCK, KNOCK, KNOCK

"Are you in there, Hadji?" Sherry asked softly. Fuzzy took a step back, looked at Hadji, and then smiled. She was enjoying the nervous look he had on his face. Fuzzy bobbed her head up and down at him, coaching him to answer Sherry.

"Yeah, baby. Give me a minute and I'll be right out." Hadji looked at Fuzzy as if asking her what next. Fuzzy looked at the door on the far side of the room and then pointed." Go," he mouthed to Fuzzy. Fuzzy raised up her pointer finger and motioned him over.

"What!" After she waved him over again, he went. Fuzzy planted another soft kiss on his lips before disappearing behind the door that led to the Jacuzzi in the next room." Damn that was close," Hadji said to himself as he made his way over to the sink to turn on the water. After a few seconds, he turned it off then opened the door.

"What were you doing in there?" she questioned, trying to look around him. She thought it was mighty odd that Fuzzy was nowhere to be found once Hadji went into the mansion. That on top of Fuzzy keeping her eye on him the entire time at the cookout made her extra suspicious. Sherry most definitely made a mental note to keep a close eye on Fuzzy from now on.

"Using the bathroom. What else would I be doing in there?" Hadji asked as he brushed past her and headed down the long hallway. Sherry stood at the entrance of the bathroom a few more seconds. She was about to turn and leave, until the door on the far side of the spacious bathroom caught her eye.

"I wonder what's on the other side of that door," she thought. Right when she was about to go find out, Hadji called out to her.

"Come on, baby!" She turned around and saw Hadji waiting on her. Giving him the benefit of the doubt, she headed down the hall in his direction and followed him out of the mansion to the car.

Fuzzy watched from her bedroom window as Hadji lifted up the passenger door of his NSX for Sherry to get in, wishing it was her getting inside. After lifting the door in the air, Hadji looked up and saw Fuzzy staring down at him. Once she blew him a kiss, she disappeared. Hadji shook his head in hopes of shaking her out of his mind, at least for the moment, and then slid into the driver's seat and started the engine. He let the whistling of the twin turbos idle out before he put the sports car in drive and headed home.

The only noise that could be heard were the sounds of K. Michelle through the surround system."

Are you fucking her?" Sherry asked out of the blue, catching Hadji completely off guard. He was glad that he had never had sex with Fuzzy, because he never lied to Sherry and didn't want to start now.

"Hell no," he answered honestly." Why would you ask me a question like that?" Even though deep down in her heart she believed her husband was telling the truth, her heart still felt a small amount of pain in it. Instead of answering Hadji's question, Sherry reached over and removed the small smudge of lip gloss that rested on the side of his mouth.

"Don't," Sherry warned as Hadji opened his mouth to try to explain. He did just that, not wanting to dig a deeper hole by trying to push the issue further. He diverted his eyes back to the road, and for the rest of the ride home neither one of them said a word.

Once Hadji pulled up at the end of the cul de sac, he drove his car into the garage and parked it between

Sherry's Honda Accord and his white-on-white Lex coupe. As soon as Hadji killed the engine, Sherry lifted her door in the air then stormed into the mansion like a mad woman. He knew not to bother her at the moment, so instead of going upstairs, he went straight to the bar to fix himself a stiff drink of premium vodka.

Three glasses later, Hadji decided to call it a night and headed upstairs." Damn," he cursed when he tried to open the locked door. Just as he lifted his fist to knock, Sherry opened the door with a pillow, a comforter, and his phone charger in her hands." It's worse than I thought," Hadji said to himself as he took the items and headed back downstairs to the living room to sleep on the couch. He knew he would be in the doghouse for quite some time. When he walked into the living room and made his bed for the night (the couch), his mind drifted back to the last time he had hurt Sherry.

One Friday when Hadji came home from meeting with his cousin Sean at the bookstore he had invested part of their money into, he noticed Sherry sitting at the foot of their bed in tears." What's wrong, baby?" he asked as he took a seat beside her and wrapped her in his arms. He figured she was having one of those days when she replayed the events of her kidnapping over in her head.

"Don't fucking touch me!" she screamed at the top of her lungs, followed by slapping his face. Sherry jumped to her feet and stormed out of the room. Hadji jumped to his feet to rush after her, when the image from the television caught his eyes.

"NOOOOO!" he screamed as he watched the scene of him fucking the stripper at his bachelor's party play out. He sat back down on the edge of his bed and buried his face in his hands. He heard the front door slam shut behind her and knew she was gone. He just hoped she wasn't gone forever.

It was almost midnight when Hadji heard the front door open. Sherry walked in their bedroom and headed straight for the shower, then shut the door behind her. Hadji made his way over to the door and tried to open it, but it was locked.

"Baby, I tried to tell you," he confessed, placing his forehead against the door. Even though he knew the door was locked, he tried to open it again." Please, baby, just let me in so we can talk about it. You know I never meant to hurt you." He said everything he could think of, but it was no use. Sherry stood under the shower head and let the water cascade from her head to her toes, crying as she listened to Hadji pour his heart out to her.

Twenty minutes later, Sherry unlocked the bathroom door and walked past Hadji with hurt in her eyes, then climbed into bed with no clothes on. Hadji followed and held her in his arms as she stared out the window." I need some time to myself, Hadji," she admitted as she gazed off at the stars." I'll gather all of my things in the morning." Sherry cried. Hadji lay there motionless as he let her words sink in. At that moment, Hadji felt like his entire world had come tumbling down on him. He closed his eyes and kissed the back of Sherry's head.

"I can't let you do that," he objected." This is your house. I bought it for you. I'll pack my things in the morning and leave."

After snapping back to the present, Hadji did something that he hadn't done in years. He got on his knees and prayed that the Lord gave him the strength he needed to fight off the craving he had inside for Fuzzy. Once he was finished, he got off his knees, lay on the couch, and hoped that his prayers would be answered in time.

$ $ $

Fuzzy tossed and turned all night, thinking about Hadji as well until she decided to get up and take a drive. She thought long and hard before killing the engine and walking up to the door." I'm coming," she heard a voice call out. A minute later the door knob began to turn. Shelia smiled with her arms held wide after opening the door. Instead of greeting her, Fuzzy fell into her embrace face-first. Shelia was in shock. For as long as she could remember, she had never seen Fuzzy cry, besides at her father's funeral.

"Come on in, baby." Shelia shut the door behind them then led Fuzzy to the living room." You want something to drink? Water, orange juice, apple juice?" Shelia asked as she ran off a list of beverages that she had in the kitchen to drink.

"Do you have anything much stronger?" Fuzzy asked, wiping her eyes. Hearing those words brought a huge smile to Shelia's face since she was already upstairs indulging in a glass of gin and cranberry juice watching Set It Off before Fuzzy came over. Once Shelia grabbed the half-empty bottle of gin, she grabbed the rest of the cranberry juice then headed back down the stairs so they could get their drink on and relax.

"Here you go," Shelia offered, handing Fuzzy a glass of ice and the bottle of gin for her to pour her own troubles. After mixing the drink, Fuzzy downed the glass completely before placing it down in front of her and filling it back up again. "Now what's the problem?" Shelia questioned, ready to find out what was bothering her niece.

"It's—" Fuzzy began, but she couldn't find the right words to explain what was on her mind.

"It's Hadji and?" Shelia cut in and finished her sentence for her. Fuzzy looked over at Shelia surprised.

"How did you know?"

"Girl, please. I could tell you were feeling him by the way you were checking him out at the cookout when you thought no one was looking at you," Shelia giggled, ready to get the 411 on the two. Fuzzy didn't think anyone saw her. She hoped Hadji's wife didn't notice. Not that she was afraid or anything like that, she just didn't want Hadji to get into any trouble at home. She was snapped out of her thoughts by the sound of Shelia's voice. "I'm sure I don't have to tell you that it's a dangerous game you're getting yourself into." Shelia watched Fuzzy's brow raise and her forehead wrinkle. "Not saying that you can't handle yourself, but Sherry has killed before as well, and you know as well as I do, once you killed before, you will kill again!" Fuzzy took in everything Shelia had just said to her and knew she was telling the truth.

"I'll keep that in mind," Fuzzy responded, then finished off her glass of liquor. She was glad she had stopped by Shelia's place to get her mind right. She felt like a lot had been lifted off of her shoulders. After assuring her that she would be getting back with her by the end of the week, Fuzzy headed back to the mansion. By the time she pulled up the circular driveway, she realized that he was on her mind now more than ever. "Oh well," she concluded, then went in the mansion to take a cold shower to calm the storm that had brewed up between her legs.

"Mommy, Mommy, Mommy," Sade repeated, jumping up and down on Fuzzy's bed." Will you take us to the park, PLEEEASSSE!" she begged.

Fuzzy lazily opened her eyes and focused them on her little bundle of joy before her.

"Please," she heard Jr. and Lil Menace say in unison as they both stood at the foot of her bed with pleading eyes.

"Sorry, senorita," Maria apologized, racing into Fuzzy's bedroom out of breath. She had been chasing the kids around the mansion all morning. Maria was Slim's housekeeper that played nanny to the kids whenever they came to stay with Slim, which was quite often.

She also was Mr. Biggs's housekeeper when he

was living, so she was like part of the family.

"No problem, Ms. Maria." Fuzzy waved off her apology then began to get up.

"No, no. I'll take them." Hearing those words were like music to Fuzzy's ears, because she was still a little hungover from the blast she had at the cookout the night before.

"Are you sure?" Before Maria got the chance to respond, the kids all cheered and ran out of the room to put their shoes on.

"Get you some rest, senorita. We'll be back later," Maria promised, then closed the bedroom door behind her. Fuzzy was glad she didn't have to get up right away. Now she could go back to sleep, and hopefully continue her dream where she left off at, in Hadji's arms. She smiled at the thought even though she doubted very seriously that she would be so lucky.

Even though Fuzzy wasn't lucky enough to continue her last dream where she had left off, she did dream of Hadji nonetheless. He had just slid her panties to the side and was about to put himself inside of her, until her cell phone rang, waking her from her dream." Shit," she cursed, then rolled over to pick her phone up off of the nightstand." What?" she snapped at the caller without looking at the caller ID.

"Meet me at the club," Lil Man spoke into the receiver. Fuzzy could tell by the sound of his voice that something was wrong.

"Is everything okay?"

"No. I'll fill you in when you get to Drama." After agreeing, Fuzzy ended the call and dialed up Hadji. He answered on the second ring.

"Can you meet me at club Drama in about an hour?" Once he assured her that he would be there, Fuzzy ended the call and hopped in the shower to get herself together.

$ $ $

By the time Fuzzy walked into club Drama, Hadji and Lil Man were on their second drink. "So what's going on?" Fuzzy asked as she made her way to the bar and sat her handbag on the bar's counter then poured herself a drink. She had a feeling she was going to need one after Lil Man told her what was so important.

"Meka's gone," he confessed.

"Boy, I told you to keep your dick in your pants."
Fuzzy laughed thinking about how many times she warned him about stepping out on Meka. Realizing that Hadji nor Lil Man joined in on her wisecrack, she became serious. "It's that serious, huh?" she asked, then took a sip from her glass.

"B.B. took her from our house."

"So that's why Meka didn't come to the cookout with him," she concluded as she fixed herself another drink. "I'll call Uncle Slim." Fuzzy went into her handbag to retrieve her cell, until Lil Man stopped her.

"B.B. warned that if I tell the crew or the police, Meka is dead!" Fuzzy removed her hand from her bag and tried to think of a plan to get Meka back. Coming up with nothing, she watched Hadji pull out his cell, flip through his contacts, then connect the call.

"Who are you calling?" she asked. When she got no response in return, she sat back and watched Hadji work his magic.

"I need to call in a favor," he told the caller then gave his location. "Bet, I'll be waiting on you." Ending the call and looking up into Fuzzy's wondering eyes, he answered her.

"We're going to need some high-tech shit if we intend on getting Lil Man's girl back without losing one of our own." He looked in Lil Man's eyes to make sure he had faith in his new general.

$ $ $

"Glad you two could make it," Hadji said to the twins (Malek and Maleki) when they walked into club Drama. He hated to call in a favor on such short notice, but Lil Man left him with little to no other option at the time.

Malek and Maleki were two hustlers that had come up in the game quickly, due to the fact that when they were in their teens they robbed and killed the head of the Arabian mafia for killing their father. After taking all of the drugs and money, they inherited major beef with the other head Arabs since they interfered with their money. To make things right, the twins payed the debt off, which landed them a lifetime contract with the richest and deadliest mafia on the East Coast.

"The honor is ours," Malek replied humbly.

Truth be told, the twins were glad Hadji had called in the favor, because they were hoping he would take them up on the offer and join forces with them. Even though Hadji had been out of the game for years, they knew his reach ran long and would be perfect to fit the missing spot in their puzzle.

"So what is it that you need from us, homie?" Maleki asked as Malek faded to the back to give his brother the floor. Unlike Malek, Maleki was the twin that took charge and was always ready to get his hands dirty. After Hadji ran down the situation to the twins, Maleki walked out of the club and returned five minutes later with a duffel bag thrown over his shoulder. "This should do it." He dropped the duffel at Hadji's foot then stepped back.

"My man." Hadji smiled, opening the duffel that contained enough explosives to take out four city blocks. "How much do I owe you for this?" Hadji asked, digging into his pocket. Instead of replying, the twins turned and headed for the door. "Oh yeah, one more thing." They stopped in their tracks and turned back around to see what he needed. "I need for you to trade cars with me." Malek smiled and looked at his twin brother, glad that he was able to talk him into driving one of their old cars instead of one of their new toys. Maleki reached in his pocket and threw the set of keys to Hadji. To both of their surprise, Hadji threw the keys to his Acura NSX.

"Make sure you don't drive it in the Knightdale area," he warned, not wanting Sherry to see either of them driving the wedding gift she had bought him when they returned from the honeymoon in Dubai.

"We got you," they said in unison, after catching on to what he was insinuating. Once they were out of the club, Hadji went into the bag and pulled out all of the contents.

"C-4, check; machine guns, check; tracking device, check," Hadji ran off as he took each item out and placed it on the bar counter.

After running through the plan Hadji had come up with, Lil Man promised to call them as soon as he heard from B.B., then left with the tracking device so he could put it inside the glove box in his Cadillac.

"Now what?" Fuzzy asked as she poured herself another drink.

"Now we wait for Lil Man to call us and let us know that he's heard from B.B.," Hadji answered, then lifted the bottle and took a drink straight from the bottle. He knew that being alone with Fuzzy was one big test that was put in front of him. He just hoped he could pass it.

$ $ $

Lil Man rode around the streets of Wilson in a daze. Never in a million years did he think he would know the actual day of his death. He rode through every neighborhood he could think of, remembering all the fun times, as well as the fights and shootouts he had in them. He wanted to go see his son at Meka's mother's house before he traded his life for hers, but didn't know what he was going to say to her mother because he knew she wasn't going to keep going for the lies he told. Besides, he had run out of them anyway. His phone rang, snapping him from his thoughts. "Yeah," he answered, hoping it was B.B. A wave of relief came over him when he heard the sound of Kia's voice on the other end. "I'm on my way," he replied then ended the call. After making a right at the next corner, he got on Highway 301 and headed to her apartment. He had vowed never to see or talk to her again, but since this was his last day on earth, he decided to relieve a little stress for old times' sake.

Just like every other time Lil Man pulled up to Kia's apartment, she came to the door naked and welcomed him in. She knew she had a lot of making up to do from the last time he came over and she showed her ass." Hey, baby," she cheered when he walked through the door. After nodding his head in acknowledgement, Kia followed him down the hall and up the stairs to her bedroom. To her surprise, instead of sitting on the bed and dropping his pants and taking his dick out for her to put in her mouth, Lil Man sat down, hit the bed beside him, then motioned her over. She noticed the stress lines creasing his forehead as she made her way over to him." What's wrong, Lil Man?" she asked, worried. She placed both hands on the side of his face.

"Promise me something," he asked her with a serious face.

"You're scaring me, Lil Man. What's going on?" Kia stood to her feet and hovered over him. Lil Man reached out and put her hand in his.

"Promise me!" he demanded. After she agreed, he made her promise to straighten her life up and never settle for being second in any nigga's life." You're so much better than you think you are," he assured her before his phone began to ring. A tear came to his eye, knowing who the call was coming from." Speak," he answered then listened as the caller gave him the location to meet B.B. at. When Lil Man ended the call, the tear rolled down his cheek." I gotta go." Lil Man stood to his feet and headed toward the door.

"Please don't go," Kia begged as she pulled at the back of his shirt, but it was no use. Lil Man had his mind made up and was on a mission. Kia followed him all the way to the front door. Not able to take it anymore, Lil Man turned on his heels, grabbed Kia by her throat and slammed her back hard onto the wall. Kia reached forward and wiped the tears out of his eyes then leaned forward and placed her tongue in his mouth. Lil Man kissed her back like there was no tomorrow then took a step back.

"I love you, Lil Man," she promised him.

"I love you too," he told her back then headed for his car.

If it was under any other circumstances, he would have never told Kia that he loved her, even if he did, but he knew that was the only way he would get her to let him leave. Once Lil Man started the car and put it in drive, he took one last look in Kia's direction. To his surprise, she wasn't there anymore.

As soon as he pulled out into the traffic, Lil Man picked up his cell phone and called Fuzzy.

$ $ $

Fuzzy and Hadji had ordered pizza and were in her office in the back eating and having a good conversation. She hadn't enjoyed talking to anyone as much since her and Speedy use to stay up late at night talking until the wee hours of the morning. It felt foreign to her, being able to completely open herself up to another man the way she was opening up to Hadji. "You know your father would be very proud of you right now?" he asked her out of the blue, catching her off guard.

"What makes you think that?" she questioned doubtfully, taking a sip of her drink.

"Look at you. You're running the family with an iron fist, just the way he predicted," he pointed out. Hadji smiled as he thought back to the many conversations he and Mr. Biggs had about Fuzzy one day taking over his position once Hadji turned the opportunity down for what seemed like the hundredth time.

Fuzzy smiled, also thinking of the many times she would ride out with her father when it was time for him to meet with his supplier. He instilled in Fuzzy that if anything ever happened to him, he wanted her to check his books, collect what was owed to him from everyone, then take it to his connect. So once he was killed, that's exactly what she did. Little did she know that day would change her life forever. She smiled remembering it again in full detail.

That day, she pulled her 740 BMW into the lot of the small junkyard located in the country part of Kenly, North Carolina, twenty minutes outside of the Wilson city limits. She had visited the place on several occasions, so it was nothing for her to find it.

When Fuzzy stepped out of her car, she was greeted by a burly looking Hispanic guy with a long ponytail. "I'm here to see—" she began before the burly looking Hispanic guy interrupted her.

"Yes, I know. He is expecting you," he said, then

led the way into the small building that sat off to the left. When Fuzzy entered, she noticed three men outside of the office door talking. She could tell that the tall muscular one in the white suit had to be the boss because once they looked up and saw her standing there, the other two stood in front of him like shields. "Who do we have here?'" the Hispanic male in the white suit asked with a smile on his face. He made his way over to Fuzzy and looked her over. Satisfied, he looked deep into her eyes. Being that Biggs taught Fuzzy to always look a man in his eyes, she never broke eye contact, not until she heard a familiar voice call out her name.

"Senorita Chantel," Manny called out to her as he stepped out of his office door. "I see you've met my brother, Jesus." Manny smiled then walked over to his brother and placed a hand on his shoulder.

"Unfortunately, yes!" Manny looked from Fuzzy to Jesus, and noticed the look in his brother's eyes.

"Chantel," Jesus repeated her name then reached for her hand. To Fuzzy's surprise, she didn't reject him. It was something about his touch that she kind of liked. "A beautiful name for such a beautiful woman," Jesus complimented, then placed a kiss on the back of it.

"Thank you," Fuzzy found herself saying before removing her hand from his and turning to face Manny. "Can I talk to you in private?"

"Sure," Manny answered, then pointed to his office.

"Give me a minute to speak to my brother and I'll be right in."

Fuzzy turned and headed to the office. Right before she opened the door, she turned to take one last look at Jesus. That's when he blew a kiss in her direction.

Once Manny entered the office, he gave his condolences, and within the hour, Fuzzy got connected with the most powerful drug lord on the East Coast.

The sound of Hadji's voice snapped her back to the present.

"So why is it that I never seen you come to the castle before when you came to see my father?"

Fuzzy twisted her mouth to the side doubtfully." When?" she questioned.

"When I used to meet him in his home office and he would watch you play the grand piano on the monitor." After describing things Fuzzy would wear, she knew he was telling the truth. Fuzzy sat back in her seat smiling, thinking of the little princess dress that she had to wear whenever she played at the piano." You were so adorable." Hadji smiled thinking of the young girl that played for her daddy.

"That was then and this in now," Fuzzy found herself saying defensively. It was true, Fuzzy was a little girl back then, but now she was a fully developed grown woman with needs." Now I'm all grown up," she claimed, biting down on her bottom lip as she made her way around the desk. Hadji sat stiff as Fuzzy walked behind him and whispered in his ear." Or do you think I'm still that little girl at the piano?" she asked, swallowing his whole earlobe in her mouth. Hadji closed his eyes and took in a deep breath from the warmth of her tongue.

"You definitely ain't that little girl no more," he admitted. Fuzzy glanced down at his crotch area and could see his erection growing. She reached for it the same time her cell started to ring.

"Shit," she cursed under her breath when she realized that it was Lil Man." What?" Hadji asked as he opened his eyes to see what was going on.

"That's Lil Man," she replied as she walked back around the desk to answer her phone." Okay. We're on the way!" Fuzzy replied, then ended the call." He said B.B. just called him with the location. Turn on the tracker." Hadji was glad that Lil Man called when he did, in a way, because he didn't know if he could've fought her off even if he'd tried to. Hadji stood up and took the tracker out of his pocket then turned it on. They could see the red light blinking that indicated Lil Man's whereabouts.

"Come on. He's about two minutes away from us." Fuzzy grabbed her jacket, a Beretta 9 and her Derringer and followed Hadji out of the club to the four-door Maxima that the twins left for him.

It had been a while since Chris had been in Wilson." Damn, a lot of shit done changed," she said to herself as she drove her Jaguar down Ward Blvd. She pulled into Toisnot Park to feed the ducks. That was something that she used to love to do whenever she wanted to clear her mind.

She pulled into a park in front of the playground and turned the car off. So much had happened in her life over the past few years. She lost the love of her life, as well as coming within inches of losing her very own. She shook those memories from her head and stepped out of her car. She followed the path alongside the lake in the middle of the park until she made it to the other side." I most definitely am taking the bridge back," she thought to herself, out of breath as she looked at the bridge that crossed the lake to where her car sat.

After taking a seat, she took a moment to reflect on her life. She was doing good for herself, damn good, but if she could turn back the hands of time, she would. She was lost in her thoughts until she noticed a Mercedes van pull up and three kids hop out the side of it. "It can't be," she said to herself, squinting her eyes to get a clearer view.

$ $ $

Lil Man looked up at the address above the front door of the warehouse then down at the paper in his hand. He checked twice to make sure he was at the right location. As soon as he shut his car off, his phone rang. "Yo," he answered.

"Get out the car and walk through the door in front of you," the caller demanded. He could tell that it wasn't B.B. because the caller's voice wasn't filtered like the other times. Lil Man opened his car door and stepped out.

"Here goes nothing," he said to himself as he walked the walk to his death that awaited him. When he stepped in he had to adjust his eyes to the darkness. Right when he was about to announce his presence, a cold piece of steel pressed against the side of his head.

"Put your hand in the air, nigga, and don't try no funny shit," Ant demanded." So what do we got here?" he smiled as he removed Lil Man's .357 from his waistline.

"Yo, where's my girl? I wanna see her," Lil Man demanded, turning around to face the man with the gun to his head. Lil Man stared into Ant's dark, cold eyes. The stare down lasted a few seconds until Lil Man heard the familiar filtered voice speak up.

"Bring him back here to the office," B.B. ordered Ant.

"Go."

Lil Man turned and headed to the back. An additional shove or two from Ant made the walk much quicker. As soon as Lil Man walked into the back office, Meka stood to her feet and jumped into his arms.

"Are you okay? Did they touch or harm you? He fired off question after question without giving her a chance to respond. He was so glad to see her, even if it was going to be his last time."

"No. I'm good, baby," she promised him, kissing him on the lips.

"Aww. Ain't this cute? Look at them, Ant. True love." B.B. smiled before turning serious. Lil Man and Meka unlocked lips and looked at B.B., who was ducked off in the corner dressed in all black.

"I'm here now, so let my girl go!" Lil Man could feel Meka turn and look at him, but he couldn't turn and look back at her because he knew if he did, he might do something stupid. He couldn't afford that. He had to make sure she made it out safely before Fuzzy and Hadji showed up, because he knew when they did, it was going to be like the wild wild West up in the place.

"I'm not leaving without you," Meka leaned in and whispered into Lil Man's ear to let him know that she was going to ride with him until the wheels fell off. Lil Man tried talking sense into Meka, but she was standing firm on her decision.

"You didn't actually think I was going to let her leave, did you?" B.B. grinned, taking a step closer. Once in arm's reach, B.B. drew back and slapped Meka to the ground." Stupid bitch!" Lil Man lunged for B.B.'s throat but was stuck in the back of his head with the .380 that Ant held in his hand.

"What is this really about?" Lil Man asked, rubbing the lump that had formed on the back of his head.

"It's all about REVENGE," B.B. answered, taking a step back. Lil Man stared at B.B. with a confused look on his face. He had no idea why B.B. wanted revenge on him. As far as he knew, he didn't even know who B.B. was. The fitted Nets hat, dark designer shades, and oversized hood disguised B.B.'s identity perfectly.

"Reveal yourself," Lil Man taunted in an attempt to buy a little time. Seeing that B.B. wasn't buying it, he hit a little lower below the belt." What, you a scared-ass bitch or something?" That last comment got a laugh out of B.B.

"Me, scared? That's where you're wrong," B.B. corrected." Black Beauty ain't scared of nothing."

"Black Beauty, Black Beauty," Lil Man repeated, trying to remember where he heard the name from.

"But you are right about one thing." B.B. walked up on Lil Man and removed the hood and fitted cap. Neat dreads flowed from them like water from a waterfall, but B.B.'s identity still remained a mystery. It wasn't until B.B. removed the shades and dreads that things all started to become clear to Lil Man.

He shook his head in disbelief, regretting the decision he once made. "You fuckin bitch . . ."

$ $ $

Once Maria walked into the grocery store with the kids, Chris got out of the car and went in behind them. Maria's plan was to go in and pick up the ice cream that she had promised the kids, along with a few other items, but she ran into an old friend and got lost in their conversation." Okay . . . Call me later," she told her friend thirty minutes later. After agreeing, her friend headed to the check-out counter to pay for her things. Sade, Jr., Lil Menace, where are you?" Maria called out as she passed by each aisle." There you go." She smiled when she saw Sade and Lil Menace side by side." What's wrong?" she asked when she got close and saw Sade crying.

"Jr's gone," she answered, then pointed to the store's exit. Maria grabbed Sade and Lil Menace by the hands and drug them to the exit. By the time they made it out of the store, Maria saw a mint-green luxury car peeling out of the parking lot. Rushing to the van, Maria buckled the kids in and headed straight to the only person that she knew could help her.

$ $ $

"You fuckin' bitch," Lil Man cursed, looking up into the smiling face of Tawana. "I knew I should've killed your no-good ass back in Jersey." Tawana bit down on her bottom lip and thought back to that dreadful day that Speedy came up to New Jersey and took their son Jr. from her:

Lil Man looked down on the couch at Tawana and Crystal. His heart went out to Tawana. After escaping death once he couldn't have it on his conscience to be the one to actually take her out." What are you waiting for?" Crystal shouted. Crystal, on the other hand, was a totally different story. Ever since he laid eyes on her he couldn't stand her. The only reason she was still breathing at that very moment was out of respect for Menace, because he knew how much he loved her.

"If you're gonna kill us just get it over with. I don't got shit to live for anyway. I already lost Speedy, King's dead, and now my son was just taken away from me," Tawana cried. Lil Man thought long and hard before he made his decision. He raised the gun in his hand and let the cannon sound off two times. When Tawana and Crystal realized that neither one of them were shot, they opened their eyes.

"If I ever see either one of you again, you're dead," Lil Man promised, and he meant what he had said.

"Thank you," Crystal said sincerely as Lil Man turned around and headed out the door. Tawana, on the other hand, had thoughts of revenge on her mind and wasn't going to stop until she got it, no matter who had to die to get it. Little did Lil Man know, letting Tawana and Crystal live would be his ending.

Tawana's words brought him out of his thoughts." Yeah, you should have killed us back in Jersey. Now you're gonna pay for your decision with your life." Before Tawana got the chance to pull the trigger, her cell phone rang." Keep an eye on them two," she ordered Ant as she pulled it from its clip.

"Hello."

"Mamaaaaaa," Jr. cheered into the receiver. Tawana thought she was losing her mind.

"Jr.?" she questioned. Lil Man's heart sank at the mention of Jr.'s name.

"Yes. Where you at, Mommy? I want to see you." Tears welled up in Tawana's eyes before freely flowing down her cheeks. Before she could say a word, Crystal got on the phone.

"Where you at, bitch?" she asked excitedly.

"At the old warehouse about to put this nigga and his bitch out of their misery."

"What?" Crystal asked, dumbfounded. She had tried to talk Tawana out of killing Lil Man on numerous occasions, but she would never listen.

"Look, I don't got time to argue with you right now. Meet me at the hotel in thirty minutes so we can hit the highway and go home," Tawana ordered, then ended the call before Crystal had the chance to say anything else. For some strange reason her son's voice started to make her have a change of heart. She badly wanted to kill Lil Man for violating her and her sister, as well as kill Meka, but that would make her no better than Lil Man or Speedy for taking Lil Lucky's parents from him." Let's go!"

Ant looked at Tawana like she had lost her mind." What!" Tawana walked up to Ant and looked in his eyes." I said let's go." Ant lowered his weapon and took a step back. He didn't like Tawana's decision, but what could he do? She was the boss. Once Ant walked across the room he stood at the door and waited for Tawana. She looked down and could see the hate in Meka's eyes. She just hoped she wouldn't have to deal with her later. To wipe all thoughts of revenge out of her head, Tawana turned to Lil Man and smacked him on the side of his head with her gun. She had forgotten that the hammer was cocked back, and it accidentally went off from the impact.

"Nooooo!" Meka cried out as Lil Man fell to the side with blood gushing from his head.

KA-BOOM. A loud explosion came from the front entrance of the warehouse. Ant stuck his head out of the office door and looked down the long hallway.

"Come on. We got to go. That nigga Hadji and Fuzzy just came in." Tawana knew they were outgunned and had no way of making it out alive if she decided to shoot it out with them, but what sealed the deal was the thought of holding Jr. in her arms again. Once Tawana exited the office and headed to the back exit of the warehouse, Ant fired off a few rounds to keep Hadji and Fuzzy at bay, at least long enough for her to pull the car up so he could hop in and make a clean getaway.

"Meka, Lil Man?" Fuzzy called out as she and Hadji made their way down the hall in their direction.

"We're in here," Meka called out as she cradled Lil Man's head in her lap. When Hadji and Fuzzy entered the office and saw Meka holding Lil Man's head they thought the worst." You're gonna be okay, baby," Meka whispered, rubbing the side of his face.

"Where's B.B.?" Hadji asked, looking around the room. Meka told him B.B. and Ant just went out the back exit. Hadji jetted out of the room and headed to the back exit with hopes of catching up with B.B. and Ant.

"Did you get a good look at him?" Fuzzy questioned. Meka was about to answer but looked down at Lil Man as he came to.

"You're alive," she shouted, a little too loud for

Lil Man. He grabbed his head and raised up." I thought she shot you." Lil Man rubbed the huge gash over his head.

"Nah, that bitch's gun went off when she struck me in the head with it."

"Bitch?" Fuzzy stood with a confused look on her face. Before Lil Man could elaborate on who B.B. was, Fuzzy's cell rang.

$ $ $

"Are you sitting down?" Slim asked when Fuzzy answered the phone.

"Slim, I'm very busy at the moment. Can what you have to tell me wait?

"I'm sorry, it can't, princess." Fuzzy could hear the worry in Slim's voice, which was very rare. That's why she gave him her undivided attention." Jr. is gone." Fuzzy thought she had heard him wrong, so she told him to repeat himself." You heard me correctly. Jr. is gone."

"What do you mean gone? What happened?" After he broke down what Maria had told him, Fuzzy ended the call and slammed her cell into the wall.

"What's up?" Hadji asked, re-entering the room. By Fuzzy's conversation and body language, Lil Man could tell that she just received the news of Jr. being taken.

"We'll get Jr. back," he stated hopefully.

"How did you know he was missing?" Fuzzy and Hadji both looked at Lil Man for an answer.

"B.B. received a call right before y'all came, informing her that they had Jr.

"Who is this B.B.?" Hadji asked.

"Black Beauty," Meka answered for Lil Man.

"Black Beauty!" he repeated, trying to remember the nickname.

"Yeah, that was what they used to call Tawana when she was coming up," Meka answered again.

"Impossible!" Fuzzy shouted." Speedy told me that Lil Man killed her and her sister when they went to Jersey and took his son from her." She looked at Lil Man for clarity." He said you killed them!"

Lil Man broke eye contact and looked at the ground." I couldn't," he admitted. Fuzzy's breathing quickened and her teeth gritted.

"And now my son's gone." Fuzzy tightened the grip on the Beretta 9 in her hand, raised it up, then shot Lil Man in the head.

"NOOOOO!" Meka cried out. Fuzzy turned around and walked out of the office in a zombie-like state. Hadji knew he had very little time to make a decision because the explosion from the C-4 had started a fire that was quickly making its way to the back. He walked up behind Meka as she huddled over Lil Man's dead body and put one in the back of her head as well. Even though he hated to kill a woman, he loved his freedom much more. Hadji made his way out the back exit where Fuzzy was sitting behind the wheel waiting to drive to Slim's place to get the complete story from Maria. As they made their getaway, they passed several police cars and fire trucks on their way to the burning warehouse." Damn, that was close," Hadji claimed then wiped the sweat from his brow. He looked over at Fuzzy in disbelief. The look she had on her face was calm and collected, not the one of someone that had just taken the life of a man that she once referred to as a little brother.

"What?" Fuzzy questioned Hadji once she noticed him staring a hole in the side of her face.

"What made you kill Lil Man?"

Fuzzy took her eyes off the road for a second to look at Hadji then hunched her shoulders.

"Because he lied to Speedy and told him that he killed that bitch in New Jersey, but he didn't, and now look what's happening. My fucking son is gone!" she answered, slamming her fist into the steering wheel.

Hadji could feel where she was coming from and had no choice but to respect her decision. The rest of the ride to Slim's was made in complete silence. Both of them were lost in their own thought, but little did they know, they were thinking about the same thing: each other.

Old memories of her and Mr. Biggs flooded
Fuzzy's thoughts as soon as her and Hadji
stepped out the back door of the castle that she once
shared with her father. After gaining her composure,
Fuzzy led the way onto the bridge that hovered over
the huge pond that separated them from Slim and
Maria.

Slim and Maria sat out back while Sade and Lil
Menace watched cartoons on the projector screen in
the movie room. Maria's eyes watered as she
watched Fuzzy and Hadji make their way across the
backyard in their direction. She could only imagine
the pain and hurt Fuzzy was feeling at the time. "Ms.
Maria, what happened?" Fuzzy questioned, pulling a
seat in front of her and sitting down. Maria placed
her hand in Fuzzy's and broke down the truth, from

the moment she took them to the park, all the way to her going to the grocery store and talking to an old friend, to her finding Sade and Lil Menace down an aisle looking at the exit.

After releasing Maria's hands from hers, Fuzzy ran her right hand over her face to wipe away her tears. The fact that Fuzzy knew Ms. Maria wasn't at fault and had been with the family before she had been born, made it even harder to do what she knew had to be done." I'm sorry, Maria," Fuzzy admitted, then stood to her feet, retrieved her gun from the small of her back, then put a bullet right between her eyes. Hadji watched Maria's dead body fall forward and out of the lawn chair she sat in, then looked over at Fuzzy. Slim rose to his feet, took the gun from Fuzzy's hand, and then walked up to Hadji.

"Make sure she gets home safe," Slim whispered in Hadji's ear before he went into the castle. Hadji walked over to Fuzzy and wrapped her in his arms.

"My baby is gone," she cried as she laid her head on Hadji's chest. He wanted to tell her that everything was going to be okay, but he couldn't. He knew that in their line of work death could come lurking around the corner at any given moment.

"Come on. I'll take you home," Hadji offered,

taking a step back and holding his hand out for Fuzzy to accept. After wiping her tears away, she placed her hands into his, and he led the way to the car.

Once Fuzzy gave Hadji the code to punch in, the front gate slid apart and Hadji pulled up in front of the mansion. Always being the perfect gentleman, Hadji walked over to the passenger's side and opened the door for her. "Thank you." She mustered up a smile then placed her hand in his. Hadji walked her to the door and waited for her to open the door before he attempted to leave. "Have a drink with me." Instead of waiting for Hadji to respond, Fuzzy walked into the mansion and left the door open for him to follow. "So what do you want to drink?" Fuzzy asked as she pointed behind her at the fully stocked shelves filled with different kinds of expensive liquors and foreign wines.

"I'll have a shot of White Hennessy," he answered then took a seat on the barstool at the bar. Fuzzy turned around and sat the entire bottle down in front of him and popped the seal. "Boy, this is going to be a long night," he thought to himself as he watched Fuzzy break the seal on the bottle of Vodka and drink it straight to the head. When she placed it on the counter in front of her, it was halfway empty.

A loud burp escaped her mouth that made her giggle.

"Sorry," she apologized, then opened a tall can of Red Bull and poured it into the bottle. Hadji made small talk in hopes of getting Fuzzy's mind off of the events that had occurred earlier on in the day. Before long they were both slurring their words and laughing at everything each other said.

"Whoa," Hadji shouted when Fuzzy tried to stand to her feet and slightly stumbled into his arms.

"I think I need to lay down," Fuzzy admitted, resting her head on Hadji's shoulder. Hadji lifted her up in his arms.

"Which way is your bedroom?" Instead of giving him the direction to the stairs, she told him to walk into the closet. Hadji looked at her strangely but did as he was told. When they made it into the closet, Fuzzy directed him to the back, where she placed her hand on an electronical pad, and a small section of the wall slid to the side.

"This is some real-life 007 shit," Hadji thought himself when the elevator door slid open. Once inside, Fuzzy pressed the number two and the door closed.

"I hate that shit," Hadji mumbled under his breath when the elevator first started to ascend upward. Feeling a little dizzy, Fuzzy let out a soft moan." Don't throw up on my shirt," he joked. Fuzzy playfully bit Hadji on his earlobe. Little did she know, that was one of his weak spots.

DING, the elevator sounded, alerting them that they had reached their destination. When the elevator opened, Hadji was at a loss of words. He carried Fuzzy over to the circular California king-sized bed and laid her down softly. Once he stood back up, he looked up and took in all of the beautiful paintings on the wall. The first one that caught his eye was the picture of Speedy and Fuzzy on their wedding day. He had to admit, Speedy was wearing the hell out of his Armani Express tuxedo, even though Fuzzy took the cake. He didn't know what kind of dress she had on, but there was one thing he knew for sure, it caressed every one of her perfect curves. He looked back over to the bed and saw Fuzzy struggling to get out of her skin-tight 7 jeans and tried to control his laugh." Are you gonna help me or stand over there laughing at me all night?" she asked in an irritated tone. Hadji choked back his laugh the best he could and walked over to the bed to assist Fuzzy with her struggle. Hadji couldn't help but notice the moistness of her Victoria's Secret panties.

"Damn, she wetter than a muthafucka," Hadji said to himself trying to keep his hormones under control. Hadji took a step back when he was finished and watched Fuzzy lift her shirt over her head." Will you look in that top drawer and hand me a T-shirt?" Hadji managed to look away and walk over to the dresser on the other side of the room to fetch the T-shirt. When he turned around, he had the surprise of his life. Fuzzy stood at the foot of the bed butt naked. Seeing that Hadji was going to need a little assistance, she walked over and took the T-shirt out of his hand.

"Thank you." She smiled then kissed him on the lips. He watched Fuzzy pull the T-shirt over her head and walk back over to the bed." You gonna tuck me in?" Hadji knew it was a deadly game that he was about to play, but how could he resist? Hadji staggered over to the bed and placed the covers on top of her.

"I got to go," Hadji said, fighting off his inner demons. As badly as he wanted to feel Fuzzy's insides, he couldn't find it in his heart to hurt Sherry, and Fuzzy understood that.

"Can you at least hold me until I fall asleep?"

Hadji thought long and hard before he gave in.

He needed to sober up if he intended on making it home in one piece. After agreeing, Hadji lay on top of the covers beside her." You okay?" he asked when he heard Fuzzy sniffling.

"I miss him." Hadji didn't know if she was referring to Jr. or Speedy. Either way he held her tighter to console her. Before long they were both out for the count, calling the wolves.

$ $ $

"OH SHIIT," Hadji cursed himself when noticed where he was at. "Sherry is gonna kill me!" Hadji threw the covers from on top of him and found himself in nothing but his boxers. "We couldn't have!" he tried to convince himself. He reached over to find out if he and Fuzzy had sex last night, but she was gone. The only thing that was on her side of the bed was a note written in lipstick that read:"I didn't want to wake you, but I had to step out for a minute to handle a few things. I'll bring breakfast on my way back in. I'll be back shortly. A toothbrush and all the necessary toiletries are in the bathroom. —Fuzzy."

Hadji reached down, got his jeans off of the floor, and grabbed his cell phone."Fuck!" He powered his phone back on and noticed that he had twenty missed calls from Sherry as well as five text messages. Right when he thought it couldn't get any worse, his voice mail indicator started alerting him. By the beeps, he could tell that he had over fifteen voice messages, all which he knew were from his wife.

After Hadji got dressed, he found his way back down stairs. "Damn this shit is big as hell," he said to himself as he walked down the long hallway toward the front door. It was like everything started to move in slow motion to Hadji. Once he made it to the double doors and pulled them open, his heart dropped and his mouth fell wide open in shock. Sherry stood before him with tears running down her face and a heart full of pain. What shocked him the most was when he looked down at her right trembling hand and saw the gun that he had purchased for her a few years ago. He knew that she was well aware of how to use it because he took her to target practice for months.

He had no idea of how he was going to explain the predicament he had found himself in, but he damn sure was about to try. "I-I-I-," he began to stutter, but Sherry raised her hand up high and silenced him. CLICK-CLACK!

Text Good2Go at 31996 to receive new release updates via text message.

–

To order books, please fill out the order form below:
To order films please go to www.good2gofilms.com

Name:_____

Address:_____

City:_____ State:_____ Zip Code:_____

Phone:_____

Email:_____

Method of Payment: Check   VISA   MASTERCARD

Credit Card#:_____

Name as it appears on card:_____

Signature:_____

Item Name	Price	Qty	Amount
48 Hours to Die – Silk White	$14.99		
A Hustler's Dream - Ernest Morris	$14.99		
A Hustler's Dream 2 - Ernest Morris	$14.99		
Black Reign – Ernest Morris	$14.99		
Bloody Mayhem Down South	$14.99		
Business Is Business – Silk White	$14.99		
Business Is Business 2 – Silk White	$14.99		
Business Is Business 3 – Silk White	$14.99		
Childhood Sweethearts – Jacob Spears	$14.99		
Childhood Sweethearts 2 – Jacob Spears	$14.99		
Childhood Sweethearts 3 - Jacob Spears	$14.99		
Childhood Sweethearts 4 - Jacob Spears	$14.99		
Connected To The Plug – Dwan Marquis Williams	$14.99		
Connected To The Plug 2 – Dwan Marquis Williams	$14.99		
Connected To The Plug 2 – Dwan Williams	$14.99		
Deadly Reunion – Ernest Morris	$14.99		
Flipping Numbers – Ernest Morris	$14.99		
Flipping Numbers 2 – Ernest Morris	$14.99		
He Loves Me, He Loves You Not - Mychea	$14.99		
He Loves Me, He Loves You Not 2 - Mychea	$14.99		
He Loves Me, He Loves You Not 3 - Mychea	$14.99		
He Loves Me, He Loves You Not 4 – Mychea	$14.99		
He Loves Me, He Loves You Not 5 – Mychea	$14.99		
Lord of My Land – Jay Morrison	$14.99		
Lost and Turned Out – Ernest Morris	$14.99		
Married To Da Streets – Silk White	$14.99		
M.E.R.C. - Make Every Rep Count Health and Fitness	$14.99		

Money Make Me Cum – Ernest Morris	$14.99		
My Besties – Asia Hill	$14.99		
My Besties 2 – Asia Hill	$14.99		
My Besties 3 – Asia Hill	$14.99		
My Besties 4 – Asia Hill	$14.99		
My Boyfriend's Wife - Mychea	$14.99		
My Boyfriend's Wife 2 – Mychea	$14.99		
My Brothers Envy – J. L. Rose	$14.99		
My Brothers Envy 2 – J. L. Rose	$14.99		
Naughty Housewives – Ernest Morris	$14.99		
Naughty Housewives 2 – Ernest Morris	$14.99		
Naughty Housewives 3 – Ernest Morris	$14.99		
Naughty Housewives 4 – Ernest Morris	$14.99		
Never Be The Same – Silk White	$14.99		
Stranded – Silk White	$14.99		
Slumped – Jason Brent	$14.99		
Supreme & Justice – Ernest Morris	$14.99		
Supreme & Justice 2 – Ernest Morris	$14.99		
Supreme & Justice 3 – Ernest Morris	$14.99		
Tears of a Hustler - Silk White	$14.99		
Tears of a Hustler 2 - Silk White	$14.99		
Tears of a Hustler 3 - Silk White	$14.99		
Tears of a Hustler 4- Silk White	$14.99		
Tears of a Hustler 5 – Silk White	$14.99		
Tears of a Hustler 6 – Silk White	$14.99		
The Panty Ripper - Reality Way	$14.99		
The Panty Ripper 3 – Reality Way	$14.99		
The Solution – Jay Morrison	$14.99		
The Teflon Queen – Silk White	$14.99		
The Teflon Queen 2 – Silk White	$14.99		
The Teflon Queen 3 – Silk White	$14.99		
The Teflon Queen 4 – Silk White	$14.99		
The Teflon Queen 5 – Silk White	$14.99		
The Teflon Queen 6 - Silk White	$14.99		

The Vacation – Silk White	$14.99		
Tied To A Boss - J.L. Rose	$14.99		
Tied To A Boss 2 - J.L. Rose	$14.99		
Tied To A Boss 3 - J.L. Rose	$14.99		
Tied To A Boss 4 - J.L. Rose	$14.99		
Tied To A Boss 5 - J.L. Rose	$14.99		
Time Is Money - Silk White	$14.99		
Two Mask One Heart – Jacob Spears and Trayvon Jackson	$14.99		
Two Mask One Heart 2 – Jacob Spears and Trayvon Jackson	$14.99		
Two Mask One Heart 3 – Jacob Spears and Trayvon Jackson	$14.99		
Wrong Place Wrong Time – Silk White	$14.99		
Young Goonz – Reality Way	$14.99		
Subtotal:			
Tax:			
Shipping (Free) U.S. Media Mail:			
Total:			

Make Checks Payable To:
Good2Go Publishing
7311 W Glass Lane,
Laveen, AZ 85339

CPSIA information can be obtained
at www.ICGtesting.com
Printed in the USA
LVOW13s1614150318
569991LV00010B/671/P